# "I'm trying to think how I can best show my appreciation, Lucy."

At Judd's obvious interest, Lucy felt bolder than ever. She shot him what she hoped was a sexy look from where she lay on the floor. "You can't do it from up there."

He knelt down. "How about from here?"

"I think you'll have to come closer."

In a blink he was only inches away from her, effectively pinning her to the floor. She could feel the heat radiating from his body, and she could even smell the subtle scent of soap and shampoo, mingled with his own unique scent that made her dizzy and giddy all at the same time.

"I should tell you, as a rule I don't sleep with guests at the ranch."

The breath went out of Lucy's lungs. "I'm the exception?" she whispered.

"You're my weakness."

He leaned closer, his hands sliding around her waist. He kissed her, creating swirling, tingling sensations all through her.

She could only hold on to him for dear life and pray that she'd always remember how this felt, because Judd had surely ruined her for anyone else.

Dear Reader,

I'm thrilled to introduce to you my first book for Harlequin Temptation, *Some Like It Sizzling*. Writing for Harlequin is a dream come true for me. Ever since I was a preteen girl sneaking my mother's romance novels off the shelves to read, I've loved the kind of stories I now have the opportunity to write.

The idea for this story came to me one sizzling-hot summer day when I let my mind wander. Maybe it was the heat, but suddenly I found myself wondering what might happen if a woman came home to find a gorgeous stranger handcuffed to her bed. How would she react? Who would this stranger be, and how would he have ended up on her bed?

Oh, the possibilities! My imagination ran wild, and I ended up with Lucy and Judd's story. These two lovers quickly worked their way into my heart and took on lives of their own with their sexy antics at the Fantasy Ranch. I hope you enjoy them as much as I did, and I hope their romance turns your cold January into a sizzling one!

I would love to hear what you think of the story. You can write to me at Harlequin Enterprises Ltd., 225 Duncan Mill Road, Don Mills, Ontario M3B 3K9, Canada or visit my Web site at www.jamiesobrato.com.

Sincerely,

Jamie Sobrato

# Some Like It Sizzling
## Jamie Sobrato

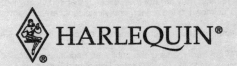

# HARLEQUIN®

TORONTO • NEW YORK • LONDON
AMSTERDAM • PARIS • SYDNEY • HAMBURG
STOCKHOLM • ATHENS • TOKYO • MILAN • MADRID
PRAGUE • WARSAW • BUDAPEST • AUCKLAND

To my wonderful husband, Rich Sobrato. Without your
unflagging optimism and encouragement, I never
would have fulfilled my dream of becoming an author.
I owe you a lifetime of steamy love scenes.

ISBN 0-373-69111-4

SOME LIKE IT SIZZLING

Visit us at www.eHarlequin.com

**Printed in U.S.A.**

"...So THEN I took off my dress and hopped into the fountain."

Lucy Connors leaned forward in her chair, hanging on her friend's every word, unable to resist the lure of Claire Elliot's tale. "What did he do?"

"He took off his shoes, jumped in—" Claire paused, stirring cream into her coffee "—and we made wild passionate love right there in the middle of the park."

She had a more exciting love life than Lucy could ever hope to have. Handsome men, scandalous rendezvous, extravagant weekend-long dates—Claire was a walking nighttime soap opera. Even her blazing red hair suggested a wildness that Lucy's mousy brown mop couldn't hope to match.

At least Lucy had her fantasies... She closed her eyes for a brief moment and imagined herself, wet and splashing in a park water fountain late at night with a gorgeous stranger. Of course, *her* gorgeous stranger would be wearing a Stetson, and he'd be tugging off a pair of cowboy boots and a faded pair of jeans to hop into the fountain with her.

Mmm...

Then reality came crashing in. She hadn't gotten within five feet of a man fit for a fantasy since the last time the UPS guy came to her door and had her sign for a delivery. Lucy's eyes popped open and she glared at the remains of her salad.

Claire frowned and reached across the table to take Lucy's hand. "Oh, sweetie, don't feel bad. You'll be having wild passionate sex again soon."

"Again?" Her past sex life could have been better described with words like "predictable" and "safe"—never wild, and rarely passionate.

Claire gasped. "Don't tell me you've never had—"

"Not wild *and* passionate. No."

"Not even once?"

"Do fantasies count?"

"You're worse off than I thought. You need to let loose! You've got this hot fantasy life and you've never once acted on it."

Lucy glanced around, hoping no one had overheard. She lowered her voice to say, "It's not that I haven't tried. But after you-know-who giggled when I did my striptease for him..."

Claire rolled her eyes. "He was a pig."

Nodding in agreement, Lucy gazed out the window next to their table and watched wilting business people hurrying to and from their cars in the oppressive Phoenix heat. Was there a single man in this entire city who could be happy with plain, boring, old her?

Their waiter appeared at the table. "Should I bring dessert now?" he asked Claire.

"Yes, please."

"Dessert? I'm too stuffed for dessert."

Claire dismissed her protest with the wave of a French-manicured hand, and the waiter cleared their lunch plates and left.

When, moments later, the entire staff of the restaurant converged on their table singing "Happy Birthday," Lucy understood. Their waiter set a small strawberry and chocolate torte ablaze with candles in front of Lucy.

When the singing stopped, the restaurant staff dispersed and Claire said, "Make a wish!"

She produced a camera and aimed it at Lucy, then started snapping photos of Lucy's startled expression.

It wasn't exactly her birthday yet. That wasn't until tomorrow, but this was her last chance to celebrate with her best friend before Claire had to leave for out-of-town business meetings over the weekend.

Lucy closed her eyes, made her wish and blew out the candles. She had learned long ago not to make outlandish birthday wishes. Better to wish for something sensible, something safe, something that could possibly come true. And after last year's disaster, the safest, most sensible wish she could produce was that she never get dumped by another fiancé at her own birthday party.

"Come on, give me a hint about what you wished for," Claire said. "If I guess it on my own it can still come true."

"Who made up that rule?"

"I did, just now."

"Trust me, you don't want to know what I wished. You'd be disappointed."

"Oh, sweetie, you just don't seem happy. Where's the spark in your life? The fun?"

"Um, I like my job," Lucy offered lamely.

But becoming a travel agent hadn't made her life

more exciting, the way she'd hoped it would when she'd changed careers a year ago. She just didn't know how to lead an exciting life the way Claire did. Lucy had been playing it safe for so long, she couldn't remember *how* to take a risk.

Claire got that little crinkle between her eyebrows that always meant she was cooking up trouble. "I *dare* you to do something totally wild, totally un-Lucy-like, in honor of your birthday."

Lucy's stomach flip-flopped. "No way. I know better than to accept one of your dares."

Claire gnawed on her lower lip, which had somehow managed to remain uniformly crimson throughout lunch. After a few moments of devious thought she said, "We'll see about that."

"What's that supposed to mean?"

Claire glanced at her watch and her eyes grew wide. "I have to be at a meeting downtown in thirty minutes." She stood, dug her wallet out of her purse, and put enough money on the table to cover both their lunches. "I'm sorry I have to rush off. I'll talk to you tonight before I leave, though, okay?"

She headed for the door, but a few feet away from it she paused, turned, and flashed Lucy a thoroughly wicked grin. "Your birthday present—I almost forgot!"

"What?"

"It will be waiting for you on your bed when you get home." Claire turned back to the door and hurried out.

Lucy waved at her friend's retreating back. Waiting for her on her bed? Claire knew where Lucy kept her emergency key, so she guessed her friend had bought her something too large or cumbersome to carry around. Probably that new comforter set she'd been eyeing in the Spiegel catalog.

She smiled and took a tiny bite of her birthday cake. Yes, the pink rose comforter set would be the perfect birthday gift, and Claire always knew just what to give.

The sweet dessert brought her taste buds to life. She closed her eyes and moaned. Oh, she couldn't even remember the last time she'd tasted it. Just for today, she'd allow herself to eat the entire miniature cake. Yes, and that would even fulfill Claire's dare!

She was doing something totally wild and un-Lucy-like already, with Claire barely out the door. Her friend would be proud.

## 1

HE WAS HALF NAKED and handcuffed to her bed. Lucy stared at the sleeping cowboy, unable to move or to even utter a cry of protest.

Everything else about her Friday had so far been normal. She'd put in a twelve-hour shift at Sunny Horizons Travel Agency dealing with frantic last-minute vacation planners and all the other customers her co-workers didn't want to handle. She'd had lunch with Claire—the one bright spot in her day—and she'd stopped at the bank machine and the gas station on her way home. Now it was time to relax and watch TV, maybe balance her checkbook and do some laundry.

But...there was this stranger wearing a Stetson and silver handcuffs. Where had he come from and what was he doing on her bed?

For one horrifying moment Lucy wondered if she'd somehow stumbled into an intimate scene about to unfold in someone else's apartment. Muscle-bound men didn't fall asleep on *her* bed, and she didn't own a pair of handcuffs.

But it was her bed, and her room, and her apartment, she assured herself as she looked around at the familiar setting. That didn't change the fact of the slumbering, handcuffed cowboy.

Long muscular arms stretched over his head and a white Stetson tipped forward covered his face. Impossibly wide shoulders tapered to a smooth torso that begged to be touched by a woman's hands. Faded jeans hugged narrow hips and enveloped bulging thighs. The picture was made complete by a pair of white snakeskin boots, accented by what looked like silver spurs.

In the agonizing moments it took her to recover from the shock, a voice in Lucy's head screamed, *Call 911!* Yet she stood in the doorway, paralyzed, unable to look away. Somehow, by some bizarre stroke of luck, here was her fantasy come to life—a real, live, hunk of a cowboy in her bedroom at her mercy. Her tired body was suddenly awake and on alert, her libido kicking into overdrive and sending tingles to places that had been dormant for months.

Her heartbeat thudding in her ears, she willed herself to run, but she couldn't move.

If she hadn't felt so numb, she might find some humor in the bizarre scene, but she'd spent the last two hours at work dealing with the very angry Mr. Dorfler, whose vacation on the Family Fun Ship had been marred by a belligerent cruise ship employee in a Loopy the Cat costume. Now all she really wanted was to slide into her fuzzy pajamas and to watch TV reruns of *I Love Lucy*.

Something, some important fact she seemed to have forgotten, was nagging at her. And then she remembered... Claire had said she'd leave Lucy's birthday gift in her apartment.

*It will be waiting for you on your bed....*

Suddenly it all made terrible sense...and she was going to kill Claire Elliot.

Easing out of the room for fear of waking the cowboy before she knew for sure that he was indeed her gift and not some masochistic intruder, Lucy rushed to the phone in the kitchen and hit the auto-dial button for Claire's number. The phone rang, and her friend picked up after two rings.

"Are you insane?"

"Hi, Luc. I presume you've found your birthday gift." Claire's self-satisfied smile was apparent even over the phone.

"If you're speaking of the Western-style gigolo or whatever he is, I found him."

Her friend's raspy laughter came across the phone line loud and clear. "He's not a gigolo, but I'm sure he'd be willing to accommodate a pretty girl like yourself during his off hours—"

"Claire!"

"He's your escort to the ranch. Didn't he explain that?"

"He hasn't quite had a chance yet, since he's currently sawing wood in my bedroom."

"Excuse me?"

"He's asleep! Now, what's this ranch you're talking about?"

"Oh, dear. I didn't realize you'd be working so late. I had him arrive there at five o'clock," Claire said, ignoring Lucy's question. "The poor guy's been handcuffed to your bed for over three hours—and what did you think of the handcuffs, by the way? Those were my idea."

"What *ranch?*" By the time she got the words out, a horrible thought had occurred to her. *The Fantasy Ranch.* The infamous adults-only resort several hours out into the desert where party people like Claire loved to vacation. Rumors of the wild parties and sexual escapades that took place at the resort circulated constantly around Phoenix. Just last month there'd been a story in the gossip pages about a party at the ranch that had ended with a fight between a popular movie actor and the paparazzo who'd caught him on camera literally with his pants down.

They'd gotten a fax at the travel agency several weeks ago saying that the ranch's end-of-summer celebration was fast approaching. It would be just like Claire to book her a surprise vacation at such an outrageous place.

Claire sighed over the phone. "I wish I could go with you. That was the plan, but these weekend meetings came up at the last minute—"

"We can go on a trip together anytime. When you get back we can plan that trip to Hawaii we've been talking about. In the meantime, I'm just going to spend the weekend watching reruns—"

"No, you're not. As your boss, I order you to take the trip as planned. Just go with Buck instead of me. You wouldn't believe what I had to go through to get him for you."

Lucy felt her insides go all jiggly as she considered the possibility of going off to a resort—an adults-only resort at that—with a complete stranger. "But I—"

"No arguments. You've said yourself that you don't want to spend the rest of your life with no one but your cats to keep you warm at night. This is your chance to learn how to loosen up and have fun. In fact, I *dare* you to be a little naughty for once in your life. And you'd better not show up at work for at least another week."

Lucy blinked in shock as the line went dead. She hit redial several times, but the line was busy. Claire had hung up on her and left her to deal with a stud named Buck. She should have never, ever told that awful woman about her secret cowboy fantasy.

After taking a deep, calming breath she crept down the hall to the bedroom again and peered around the edge of the doorway. He was still asleep—dead asleep by the sound of his slow, steady breathing.

She opened her mouth to speak, but nothing came out. What was she to say? "Hey there, cowboy, come here often?" Or maybe, "Excuse me, could you please get your boots off my bed?" There just wasn't an appropriate opener for this situation.

She allowed herself to take in the whole of him lying there with his well-tanned torso exposed, hard muscles forming a ripple effect on his abdomen, the muscles of his chest and arms bulging slightly as they strained from the handcuffs. His arms were up behind his head, his wrists clasped to the headboard with the cuffs that were looped around a wooden spindle, and the sexy thatches of dark hair under his arms were exposed. Lucy had never realized body hair could be so…arousing.

But mostly she just marveled that such a gorgeous man—gorgeous even with his face mostly hidden by the hat—was lying on *her* bed. When was the last time that had happened? Well, never. She did a quick mental inventory of all her past boyfriends, all four of them, and realized that none had been this attractive. More often than not, they'd been nice guys, but never drop-dead gorgeous. It just wasn't a quality she looked for in a man.

Not that Lucy had minded dating average-looking men. In fact, she preferred it that way. Attractive men were dangerous, arrogant, shallow, too aware of their power over women. They got what they wanted too easily, and they never noticed plain, boring women like Lucy Connors. Even if they had, she was immune to their charms.

Then why did it feel as if her whole body sighed when she took in the sight of the half-naked Buck on her bed? Why did it feel as if her pulse had centered itself between her legs? And why was there a thin film of perspiration breaking out on her upper lip?

Lucy glanced down at herself and suddenly felt self-conscious in her buttoned-up white blouse and brown tweed skirt. She looked like an uptight bore. Her chest tightened ever so slightly as she admitted that she was exactly what everyone thought she was— a woman who didn't have the slightest clue how to have fun.

Claire's words echoed in her head. *I dare you to be a little naughty for once in your life.*

Forget Claire. She and her best friend were just different, that's all, and she didn't have to change who she was to suit that woman. No, if she wanted to spend the weekend in her flannel PJs, eating carrot sticks and unsalted, unbuttered popcorn, and watch-

ing TV as she caught up on her laundry and maybe
balanced her checkbook, then that's exactly what she
would do. Claire wasn't going to lose respect for her
just because she refused to run off to some ridiculous
hedonistic resort with a male bimbo named Buck.

Lucy made up her mind. She wasn't going to accept
Claire's silly dare. But that didn't change the fact that
she still had to get rid of Buck. She took a step into the
bedroom, then hesitated. She couldn't wake a gorgeous guy like that wearing her wallflower work outfit. No, she would slip into something a little less boring while he was still asleep, and he'd never know the
difference. When she woke the sleeping stud, at least
she would do it with her womanly ego intact.

She tiptoed several feet without making a sound,
but the closet across the room seemed a mile away; her
chest of drawers wasn't any closer. She couldn't let a
little thing like that stop her, though, she reminded
herself as she took one more tentative step and sighed
with relief when Buck continued to snore softly.

She did a mental inventory of her wardrobe, wondering which outfit best suited the occasion. What she
realized immediately was that she owned a dizzying
array of beige garments, and almost nothing that was
appropriate for waking up a stud-muffin. She stopped
in her tracks in front of the closet. There sat a black
suitcase with a hot pink bow on top and a small note
card tucked under the bow. Lucy bent and plucked
the card out, recognizing her name written in Claire's
handwriting. She opened the envelope to find a card
within that read, "This is everything you'll need for
the week, except an outfit to travel in. That, you'll find

hanging on the back of the bathroom door. Just wear it!" The words "wear it" were underlined twice. Claire had signed the note, "Love, C."

Lucy eyeballed the suitcase warily. Where her tastes ran toward conservative styles and neutral colors, Claire had a penchant for outrageous platform heels and leopard-print undergarments. It was best not to look at the contents of the suitcase right away, not when she had Buck, who could wake at any moment, nearby.

She hurried across the room as silently as possible and slipped into the bathroom, gently closing and locking the door behind her. Her heartbeat thudded in her ears. When she finally turned on the light, the outfit in front of her was worse than she could have imagined.

And she couldn't wait to try it on.

Two minutes later Lucy's work clothes were lying in a heap on the bathroom floor and she was peering over her shoulder at the reflection of her butt in a pair of skintight black pants. As many other shocks as she'd received this evening, perhaps the greatest one of all was the realization that she didn't look half bad in the outfit Claire had picked out. In fact, she might even say she looked…darned good. All those years of eating wheat bran and steamed veggies had paid off.

But whether or not she could walk out of the bathroom and allow another human being to see her like this was a different matter. She finished fastening the tiny eye-hooks on the front of the stretchy red top—red, a color she *never* wore—and slid on the black platform sandals that turned out to be a lot more comfortable than they looked, then took another look at herself in the full-length mirror on the back of the bathroom door.

Okay, she wasn't exactly blessed by Mother Nature in the chest department, but still... She inspected herself further. Not bad for an outfit that made her look like a groupie hoping to sneak backstage at a rock concert. Her hair, however, was all wrong.

She reached up and removed the pins that held her French twist in place, then ran her fingers through her light brown hair until it fell around her face in waves that hung to her shoulders. She'd never liked her hair much, especially not the mousy color that made her about as noticeable as white wallpaper, or the flyaway curls that, on bad days, gave her the appearance of having wispy little horns, but with the groupie getup, she had to admit that the tousled look went quite nicely.

She wasn't wearing a spot of makeup, but there was no time to fix herself up any more than she already had, especially when her makeup collection consisted mostly of ointments and facial cleansers—not tubes of lipstick with names like Scarlet Passion.

She had a cowboy to awaken. But as she took a deep breath and stepped out of the bathroom, her throat seized up and she felt her knees begin to buckle. What could she possibly have been thinking? She couldn't wake up this strange man and let him see her like this.

She heard Claire's voice again. *You don't want to spend the rest of your life with no one but your cats to keep you warm at night.* Lucy loved her cats, but they didn't make great bed partners. Aside from their more obvious shortcomings, Romeo hogged the bed and Juliet liked to deposit dead, mangled insects on Lucy's pillow—her feline version of fancy hotel chocolates.

With that depressing thought, she decided the least she could do for herself was be proud of the way she looked in her new outfit, even if it was only for the couple of minutes it took to get Buck out of the apartment.

Her confidence somewhat renewed, she couldn't help pausing for a moment to marvel again at the male form in all its glory. Why did such gorgeous men have to exist, to remind plain women such as herself of all they couldn't have? She decided it would be wise not to spend much more time contemplating the unfairness of it all, but she still couldn't stop staring. What she really wanted was a closer look.

It only took one more gander at that perfect expanse of chest to convince her that a closer look wouldn't hurt anyone. Besides, she'd never actually seen a half-naked hunk at close range before.

As she knelt beside the bed, a little alarm sounded in the back of her brain that she quickly shut off. This was her one chance to gawk at Buck up close, and she wasn't going to waste it. She eased her elbows onto the edge of the bed and leaned in, inhaling the scent of him—an advantage of getting close that she hadn't even considered. He smelled of something warm and woodsy and unmistakably male, and the scent was intoxicating. She closed her eyes and inhaled deeper, nearly melting as the smell overtook her.

Eyes open again, she admired the smoothness of his tanned, olive skin and the little brown nipples that were nearly flat against his chest. The only body hair he had was under his arms, and a thin, dark trail that started below his belly button and disappeared into the waist of his jeans, calling Lucy's eyes lower to the impressive bulge that filled his worn-out Levi's. She felt her jaw sag as she contemplated the size of the bulge. Were there really men out there who were *that* well endowed? If so, she'd been missing the boat. Heck, she hadn't even known the boat existed.

"Hey there, darlin'. Like what you see?"

The shock of Buck's voice sent Lucy sprawling backward, landing on her rear end with a thud as she stared up at the man she'd thought to be asleep.

"H-how l-long have you been awake?" She felt her face burn as he watched her with amused eyes.

"Since you leaned against the bed."

"Oh."

"You didn't answer my question."

Lucy found herself mesmerized by his mouth as it formed words, words she didn't want to hear at the moment because he had the sexiest mouth she'd ever seen and all she wanted to do was to find out how it would feel to kiss it. Oh, it wasn't just his mouth, but his whole face! The hat had slid back to reveal features just as stunning as those below his neck. Straight nose, strong jawline, hint of a five o'clock shadow, dark brown lashes to match his tousled dark hair.

"What question?"

"Do you like what you see?" He had a lazy smile and a deeper voice than she'd imagined.

Lucy pushed herself up from the carpet and stood, futilely trying to brush cat hair from her black pants.

Anything to hide her flaming-red face from Buck. "I was just a little shocked to find a strange man hand-cuffed to my bed, that's all."

"You're hurting my feelings, darlin'."

Lucy swallowed the acid taste of fear in her mouth and wished she could slink under the bed. She forced herself to look him in the eyes, and found that they were a most intriguing shade of pale gray. "You look quite acceptable."

"Acceptable?"

"Nice, I mean."

"Look, hon, I can call the ranch and have them send another guy if I don't meet your standards—"

"No, that won't be necessary. I mean, I'm afraid my friend—the woman who arranged for you to be here—she made a bit of an error in judgment." Her face must have turned the same color as her shirt by now. She cleared her throat in the futile hope that he'd stop staring at her so blatantly.

"What sort of an error in judgment?"

"She assumed I would agree to go on this trip, but..."

He adjusted his shoulder and winced, and she realized he must have been in pain because of the hand-cuffs.

"Oh, dear, let me get you out of those. Do you have the key?"

"It's in my right-hand pocket," he said. "Just reach in there and feel around for it."

Lucy's mouth went dry as she caught his meaning. "You mean, in your pants?"

He nodded, a smile playing on his lips.

"I don't think my hand will fit in there." She eyeballed the skintight denim and wondered how she'd gotten herself into such a predicament. *Claire.* She was going to strangle that woman.

"You could unzip them if you think that would help."

"That won't be necessary." She took a deep breath and tried not to think of the things that could possibly go wrong while fishing around in a stranger's pocket.

*What the heck? This is your one chance to stick your hand into a gorgeous man's pants.*

She lurched forward, the toe of her platform sandal catching in the plush carpet, but found her balance just in time. He didn't seem the least bit uncomfortable as she slid her hand inside his right pocket for the key. It was a tight squeeze, and she had to lean over his torso a little to get her hand at the right angle. Her position forced her to inhale that dreamy scent of his again, and for at least the second time that night she felt certain parts of her anatomy turn tingly and liquid with sensation.

But there was no key.

"Are you sure you put it in your right pocket?" She withdrew her hand and breathed a sigh of relief that she had managed not to bump certain parts of *his* anatomy.

"Hmm, maybe it was the left pocket."

Lucy glared at him as she realized that he had possibly sent her fishing in the wrong pocket on purpose, that he was actually enjoying this little game. Okay, so maybe she was enjoying it, too. Just a little.

Bracing her knees on the bed, she leaned further

across his torso and started to slide her hand into the left pocket, but that was when she noticed that the sizeable bulge she'd been admiring a few minutes earlier was situated on *that side*. Her hand froze and she became all too aware of her compromised position leaning over him, at least four inches of her bare waist exposed by the short top.

She said a silent thank-you to the genius who'd invented fat-free yogurt. At least she could rest assured there were no unsightly rolls hanging over her too-tight pants. That is, if Buck were even interested enough to notice, which she doubted.

The quicker she found the key, the quicker she could put a comfortable distance between them, so as she swallowed her fear, she plunged her hand the rest of the way into his pocket and luckily felt the edge of something hard and metal rather than that other something she was trying to avoid. She caught it between her fingers and pulled it out.

"Is this it?" She held it up for him to see, but what surprised her was that she had caught him staring at that little slit of exposed skin at her waist.

"Mmm-hmm." His gaze held a glint of teasing and she knew then that he'd only been looking because he could—just like any man would—and not out of any particular sense of admiration.

Her hands shook as she inserted the key into the lock on the handcuffs and turned it, releasing Buck from his restraints. He pushed himself up, letting out a sigh of relief as he lowered his arms and rubbed his wrists where the cuffs had been. Lucy watched him, but instead of feeling relieved that there was no longer a cowboy handcuffed to her bed, she felt a new sense of vulnerability. He was a stranger in her bedroom, and now he was no longer restrained.

He must have spotted the uneasiness in her eyes, because he said, "Don't worry, darlin'. This is my job—I don't go around preying on women."

"So what exactly is it that you do besides get handcuffed to strange women's beds?"

"I work for the ranch, doing various jobs. I normally don't come to guests' homes and handcuff myself to their beds, but your friend must like you a lot, because she made special arrangements."

"My friend's a little eccentric."

"Weren't you about to tell me about her error in judgment?"

Right, she had been, but now as she stared at Buck's glorious abdominal muscles, she couldn't remember what error in judgment she'd been about to point out. He was just so...*hot*.

Lucy imagined he got more than his share of women at the ranch. In fact, they probably threw themselves at him left and right. Women went to places like that to let loose, to get wild, and to forget about their boring everyday lives. He must have thought Lucy was one of those women looking for a good time, and the idea shocked her. After a moment, though, the idea didn't seem so strange. Why couldn't she be?

Why couldn't Lucinda Jane Connors, boringly normal travel agent, let loose and have a wild, unforgettable time? That's what Claire wanted her to do. Maybe that was even what Lucy really wanted to do.

As Buck rose from the bed and retrieved his white Stetson, settling it on his head of dark brown curls, Lucy realized that this *was* what she wanted herself to do—to go to the Fantasy Ranch and do things she'd never done before, be a party girl, drink too much and stay in the sun too long, eat sinful foods and flirt with sinful men. And maybe find a man—perhaps even one who looked like Buck—with whom to have a wild, lustful one-night stand that she'd never forget. Then Claire would never again have reason to call her boring. More important, Lucy would never again think of herself as boring.

"Something wrong?"

"Huh?"

"You looked like you were in a trance there for a minute." Buck had produced a black T-shirt from somewhere and removed his hat again to slide the shirt on. Lucy allowed herself to admire the bronze contours of his torso as he lifted his arms over his head, but she averted her gaze before he could catch her staring.

"I was just thinking about what I have to do before I can leave," she lied. "I wasn't expecting you to be here, and I didn't plan to leave until tomorrow."

"Your friend told me to tell you she asked your neighbor to feed the cats, so you don't need to worry about them."

"I haven't packed yet."

"She took care of that for you." He nodded at the suitcase across the room.

"Yes, but Claire tends to be forgetful."

"She told me you might try to repack, and I have

strict orders to make sure you just take that bag and come with me. I'm supposed to remind you about 'your possible future with cats.'"

Lucy opened her mouth to argue but then thought better of it. What about this daring new woman she wanted to become? She couldn't very well become her wearing khaki trousers and penny loafers.

"Everything you need is in the bag."

"Well, I just need to grab my vitamins out of the kitchen, and then I'll be ready to go."

"Vitamins?"

"I know Claire wouldn't have thought to pack them," she said, heading into the hallway. She stopped in her tracks. She had to learn to *think* like a wild and crazy party girl. This new and improved Lucy probably wouldn't worry about Vitamin C deficiency or osteoporosis. She resisted the urge to grab her dietary supplements, reassuring herself that after the week was up, she could always start taking them again if she didn't like her new reckless self.

"Did you get them?"

Buck appeared beside her in the hallway, the black suitcase in his left hand.

"I decided I won't need them. But let me just check to make sure Romeo and Juliet have enough food and water to last until my neighbor stops by."

After she'd given the cats several extra bowls of food and water, she joined Buck in the living room where he was inspecting the photos on her mantel with a keen interest.

"I'm ready," she announced, realizing too late that

the Lucy in those photos looked a lot more conservative than she did standing there in her groupie getup.

"Is this you?" he asked, pointing to the photo in which she stood next to a Christmas tree with Claire. In the picture, Lucy was wearing a long burgundy-and-green-plaid wool skirt and a baggy turtleneck sweater. She'd been having a particularly bad hair day and little sprigs of curly hair had escaped from her bun to poke out all around her face. She looked horribly dull, she realized as she saw the picture through Buck's eyes, but it was one of her best photos. She'd never been very photogenic.

He was still waiting for a response.

"Um, yes, that's me. Bad hair day."

"It's a nice picture."

Lucy watched for him to make a face or to otherwise indicate his sarcasm, but no, he seemed serious about the compliment. Perhaps he was a bimbo stud with exceedingly good manners.

Romeo marched into the living room and gave Lucy a belligerent look. He knew what a packed suitcase and three bowls of food meant—that his Slave Human was leaving him—and he didn't like it one bit. He let out a mournful meow, prompting her to bend to rub his back one last time before leaving.

"Sorry, but you have Juliet to keep you company. I'll be back real soon."

Buck made a move toward the cat and Romeo slipped underneath the nearest chair, eyeing the stranger with derision.

"Oh, you cowardly cat. Be a nice boy and say goodbye to Buck."

"Buck? Who's Buck?"

Lucy looked up at him, her head beginning to spin. "Aren't *you* Buck?"

He frowned and shook his head. "My name is Judd. Judd Walker."

# 2

IT TOOK JUDD A MINUTE to figure out who Lucy was talking about. And then he remembered—Buck Samson. He was the ranch's most popular employee with the female guests. Claire Elliot had apparently heard about him through word of mouth and called to request that Buck himself pick up Lucy and escort her to the ranch.

Judd's older brother Mason was the owner of the Fantasy Ranch, and in the past three months he'd been experiencing what he believed were elements of a plot to ruin his business. With the busy last weekend of summer coming up, when much of the ranch's return business was decided, Mason was anxious to ensure no disasters occurred like the ones the ranch had already experienced—tainted food at the restaurant, theft, unpleasant deliveries made to guests' rooms—and that was where Judd came in.

Mason had reason to believe that Sunny Horizons Travel Agency might be involved in the sabotage, through its connection with his vengeful ex-girlfriend. Right now he was at the height of paranoia and trusted no one, including his star employee Buck, so he'd hired Judd as his private investigator and sent him on his way to find out what he could about Lucy Connors.

So here he was in the most ridiculous undercover operation he'd ever conducted, dressed like an idiot in this sleazy cowboy getup.

"I'm Buck's replacement," he explained. "He couldn't make it to be your escort, so the owner sent me instead. Is that okay?"

She still looked confused. "It's just that Claire said your name would be Buck."

"I forgot to tell her I was replacing him. The subject of my name never came up when she let me into the apartment."

"Oh." She took a step back, obviously not thrilled to find a total stranger whose name was not Buck in her apartment.

He could understand her reluctance. "Why don't you call the ranch and speak to the owner, Mason Walker. He can confirm for you that I am indeed your escort and that I don't bite—" he forced himself to add in typical Fantasy Ranch style "—unless you want me to." He realized too late that his little act didn't help the situation, so he set down the suitcase and reached for his wallet to retrieve his brother's business card.

Lucy stared at it for a moment and then looked up at him. "Walker? Isn't that your last name, too?"

"Mason's my brother."

"Oh. Well, if you don't mind holding on a minute, I think I will call, just to be safe." She eyed him warily, and he began to feel as if he had fangs.

"Why don't I wait outside?" he offered, hoping that might help her relax.

"No, that's not necessary. It's not like I haven't already been alone with you all this time."

She sat on the sofa and dialed the number to the ranch.

Judd occupied himself looking at her photos again. Why couldn't this in-person Lucy be more like the conservative Lucy in the picture? *That* was the kind of woman he needed to spend a week with, not an obvious seductress. It was almost impossible to tell if the real-life woman and the woman in the photo were one and the same.

If he had to spend an entire week keeping an eye on Lucy, he was in big trouble. The promise he'd made to himself only a month ago would be out the window in no time flat if she kept looking at him the way she did, with those satin brown eyes of hers. He had a thing for brown eyes. A bad, bad thing. But why couldn't he run into nice, respectable women with irresistible brown eyes and made-for-sin bodies?

Instead he attracted sex kittens. He'd already promised himself—*no more wild women.* They'd brought him nothing but trouble in the first thirty years of his life, and now that he was ready to settle down, he needed someone steady, respectable, and maybe even a little bit boring.

Lucy Connors, with her natural beauty, lush pink lips, wild bedroom hair and slim little waist that begged to be gripped, was definitely not boring. And in her presence he was already forgetting that he was supposed to be conducting an investigation.

He'd had enough of red-hot lust and crash-and-burn passion. He'd been scalded one too many times. He'd nearly lost himself to women like Lucy.

Judd winced at the memory of his most notable disaster—the woman who'd cost him his career in the police force. It had been his own fault for hopping into bed with a near stranger, for letting passion rule his decision-making. He should have guessed she might have been involved with one of his co-workers by her very presence at the party full of cops where they had met, but he'd never imagined she was his own boss's girlfriend.

He had put that mistake behind him and was now well on his way to respectability. The last thing he needed was to be led back into temptation by a woman who could addle his brain with her beauty and turn him back into a man ruled by his sexual urges.

But he'd promised Mason.

He made a mental note to himself to kick Mason's ass at the soonest possible opportunity. Just like when they were kids, his brother could still get him in trouble. Only this time Judd had walked into it with his eyes wide open. He never would have agreed to the investigation if his older brother hadn't sounded as though he needed the favor so desperately. Judd hadn't seen any way to say no.

"You'll have the perfect opportunity to keep an eye on her," Mason had said. "Just pretend that maybe you're attracted to her on your off hours and she'll be putty in your hands." Mason had given him the same pleading look he'd used when they were kids to get Judd to tell their mother it had been him who'd broken two plates from the china collection.

Lucy's voice interrupted his thoughts and snapped him back to the present. "Okay, thank you very much,

Mr. Walker. Goodbye." She hung up the phone and offered Judd a crooked smile. "Your story checks out, so I guess we can go."

Judd took a deep breath and smiled at the woman that was sure to be his undoing.

NOW THAT SHE HAD A GOOD view of *Judd's* face, Lucy couldn't stop staring. He was handsome the way banana splits were delicious—decadently so, with a little too much of the good stuff. Too much beauty for one man to contain, yet he managed it somehow. Remarkably, those silvery gray eyes, that nose a plastic surgeon would be proud of, those soap-opera-hunk cheekbones, and that outrageously lush mouth all combined to make a face that was gorgeous in an unmistakably masculine way.

Lucy melted a little every time she looked at him. And that was only in the beginning. After those early moments in his presence, the full weight of the situation began to sink in... And sink in some more, bringing with it a schoolgirl giddiness that threatened to undermine her sex-kitten wannabe disguise. How could she be a cool seductress as she constantly resisted the urge to blush and giggle?

She couldn't, at least not without a little help. Her plan became clear when Judd showed her to the rear passenger seat of the sport utility vehicle and offered her the complimentary bottle of champagne and box of overpriced chocolates. She'd succeed with the assistance of alcohol.

Although the rear seat had the advantage of proximity to the vehicle's built-in bar, Lucy smiled with as much confidence as she could muster and said, "How 'bout I sit up front...and keep you company."

Judd nodded one time. "Whatever you like."

She plucked the already-opened bottle and a plastic glass from his hand, eyeballing the box of chocolates he also offered with apprehension. Boring Lucy would never succumb to the wanton calorie binge that gold foil box of sin represented, but she had the feeling Wild-and-Crazy Lucy would relish every bite without thinking twice about the health conse-quences. It had been so long since she'd eaten real chocolates, she could barely remember their flavor.

"I'd better take those, too. Champagne makes me hungry." She took the box with her free hand and tucked it under her arm before climbing into the front seat.

A little alcohol-induced courage was just what she needed to get the vacation started right, Lucy told her-self as she promptly filled and emptied the cham-pagne flute twice. Since they hadn't even started mov-ing yet, she was thankful when Judd climbed into the driver's seat and studiously ignored the suddenly emptier champagne bottle that sat in the little cooler between their seats.

"Ready to go?" His gaze stopped for a moment at her shoulder, and she imagined he was checking to make sure she was buckled in, an act she found incon-gruously charming.

*He's doing it for insurance purposes,* the librarian voice in her head pointed out.

"Ready and willing," she blurted, feeling her face heat up.

Okay, so she needed a little more champagne. Problem was, she had no idea how many glasses would produce the desired confidence without bringing with it the stumbling drunkenness she hoped to avoid. Too bad alcoholic beverages didn't come with recommended dosages like prescription medications. *For increased confidence, take three eight-ounce servings every four to six hours.*

But they didn't, so she realized her plan had a big chance of backfiring. Especially since she normally didn't drink. Lucy had heard all about Claire's drunken escapades, though, so she knew it was an accepted thing for party girls to drink a little too much champagne now and again. If things got out of hand, she could always explain it away later as her way of getting rid of the stress of the workweek.

As Judd pulled out of her apartment building's parking lot, Lucy downed her third glass, and a few minutes later she was wrapped in a fuzzy sense of well-being the likes of which she couldn't remember. It occurred to her as she peered at her tantalizing driver from across the darkened cab that her plan needed another step to be complete.

Seduce Judd Walker. What the heck. If she could pick any birthday present in the world, at that moment he was what she most wanted.

She wanted to touch him, to taste him, to feel their limbs tangled together in bed. She wanted to make love to him all night, then wake up and do it again in the morning. It was the most outrageous idea she'd ever had. And possibly the most brilliant.

She opened the box of chocolates, picked one out, and took a big, sinful bite.

JUDD DIDN'T HAVE REASON yet to suspect Lucy was anything but a woman taking a vacation. He realized with a little pang of guilt that he'd already let his attraction to her cloud his reasoning. He didn't *want* her to be guilty of anything clandestine.

Before calling in Judd to investigate, Mason had figured out on his own that all the sabotage so far had taken place while employees of the Sunny Horizons Travel Agency, where Lucy worked, were staying at the ranch. And he'd made that connection because the travel agency was owned by the same corporation that owned the resort's biggest competitor, the Oasis Spa and Resort, also the same corporation run by Mason's slightly psycho ex-girlfriend.

It sounded more than a little far-fetched to Judd, but he had to agree with his brother that it was all they had to go on so far.

Judd peered over at Lucy for a moment, wondering if she'd had enough to drink yet to get loose-lipped and slip him some helpful information. "You enjoy being a travel agent?"

"How did you know what kind of work I do?"

"I did my homework, checked out your guest bio. Said you're celebrating your birthday, right?"

"Right. What's there to celebrate? Getting another year closer to death?"

"Gee, you look like you're all of what? Twenty-four, twenty-five years old? I'd say you better invest in a burial plot now before it's too late."

She laughed softly. "You get paid to say nice things like that."

"So how old are you?"

"Twenty-nine, as of tomorrow."

"Why the bad attitude?" He heard the sound of more champagne being poured into her glass. "I'm almost thirty-one, and trust me, it's not as bad as it sounds."

"This is sort of a forced celebration. I wasn't planning to go on the trip, even after I found you handcuffed to my headboard."

He hadn't been a tempting-enough invitation? Judd considered that his first impression of her as a wild party girl might not have been totally accurate. Some of the facts formed a different picture—Lucy's sedately decorated apartment, her worry over whether to pack vitamins, her affection for her two overweight cats. The contrasts formed a puzzle he could hardly wait to solve.

"Your friend Claire's the enforcer?"

"Yep."

"What made you change your mind and come with me?"

She was silent for several moments, and he began to think she wasn't going to answer, but then she said with a little laugh, "The cats. Definitely the cats."

"I guarantee you won't regret coming." What the hell did he say that for? He made it sound as if he personally was going to ensure that she had a great time.

"How did you get involved in this field?" she asked.

"This field?"

"I mean, did you set out to work at a resort?"

"No, I just sort of stumbled on the job. Mason offered it, and I accepted."

She probably thought he was an air-headed male bimbo using his body to get by in life. He wasn't sure why that bothered him so much, but it did. He'd worked hard to make his private investigation business a success and was a damn good cop before that. Whatever he accomplished in life, he didn't want to do it relying on his looks.

Judd took a mental inventory of all the ridiculous things Mason had told him would be part of his "duties." To be able to watch Lucy in a variety of settings, his brother had given him the job of fill-in, which meant he went wherever help was needed, or more accurately, wherever Mason decided he would be needed at the moment.

Mostly, he was supposed to hover nearby in the guise of making sure Lucy was happy, watching her for clues of her involvement in a plot to ruin the ranch. During the times when she wanted to be left to herself, he had to keep up the facade of being a regular employee by performing a few of the other duties. Duties he'd hotly protested, such as leading karaoke, making sure the nightclub stayed hopping at all hours of the night and joining in the "wet boxers" contest when there weren't enough entrants... Judd gripped the leather steering wheel tighter as his temper flared.

When Mason had bought a failing resort and claimed he'd wanted to turn it into an adults-only playground, Judd thought it was a stupid idea. But his brother was confident that the Fantasy Ranch would be a sure moneymaker, and he'd been right. Judd still couldn't understand the appeal of the place, especially not when things got out of hand as often as they did. Mason, however, thrived on the constant challenge.

It quickly became clear that Lucy wasn't much of a drinker. The champagne had gone straight to her head, and now when she spoke, her words slurred together slightly. When he'd glanced over at her a few minutes earlier, she'd been listing to the right in her seat, as if they were going around a sharp curve, but the road was dead straight. Judd was about to ask her if she'd had enough to drink when a low, soft moan came from her side of the Suburban. And another moan, this time louder.

His body responded primitively, and he shifted in his seat, afraid to look over to see what exactly was the cause of the moaning.

"This is incredible," she said, a little breathless.

Judd took a quick mental inventory. The leather seats? They were comfortable, but not moan-worthy. The scenery? It was pitch-black outside. Must have been the champagne then. But why the delayed reaction?

And then he caught the scent of chocolate in the air. She'd tried another one, and as he glanced over, he saw her head tilt back and her eyes close in silent rapture. She had a streak of chocolate on her lower lip.

"You're a big chocolate fan, huh?"

"I am now." She bit into another truffle and groaned deep in her throat.

"Something special about those chocolates?"

"It's just that," she said with her mouth full, pausing to swallow, "I really never eat chocolate. So many empty calories, such high fat content—"

"So you're one of those health fanatics?"

"I'm not a fanatic, I just believe in proper nutrition."

"Even on vacation?"

"Mmm, raspberry," she moaned, ignoring his question. "Oh, this is so good, why can't carrots come with raspberry filling? Want to try one?"

"I'll take that as a no."

"Hmm?"

"Never mind." He shook his head, smiling in spite of himself.

She must have finished the box, because a few moments later Judd heard it hit the floor with a soft thud.

"You know, chocolate, I think, is like sex for a woman, only better."

Judd raised an eyebrow. "This from a woman who claims never to eat chocolate?"

"Hey, I just ate a whole box of the stuff, didn't I? Besides, I have friends who eat it all the time, and I see what it does for them."

"And what is that, exactly?"

She emitted an inexplicable gush of giggles. Once she recovered, she said, "It's pure pleasure without the frustration. Like getting an orgasm every time. No worry about whether he's going to be too fast, or too distracted, or too self-absorbed..."

"I think you've had a little too much to drink. And you've definitely been meeting the wrong kind of guys."

She succumbed to another giggling fit, and Judd

took note of her laughter. It sounded...nice. Not at all the throaty seductress laugh he'd imagine her having.

"I have, haven't I?"

He decided not to ask if she was agreeing to one of his statements or both.

"I bet you get a lot of crazy drunks at the ranch." She pushed herself up in her seat and deposited an empty champagne flute in the nearest cup holder. "That must make your job more interesting—or difficult."

Judd had heard his brother's stories of the guests' antics, some of which were legendary. "Well, there was the time a woman somehow managed to get her head stuck between the legs of the cowboy statue in the cactus garden. She was, um, not wearing any clothes at the time."

"Not even underwear?"

"Not even a smile."

"Wow."

"Yeah, that's what the firemen said when they got there. And that's how the cowboy statue came to be known as One-Legged Joe."

They rode in a silence occasionally broken by Lucy's drunken giggles as Judd turned off the highway and drove along the road that led to the resort. But around the last bend they were forced to stop in the middle of the road to accommodate a pair of lovers who'd sprawled themselves across it in a sort of *From Here to Eternity* scene, minus the beach.

"What the—" Lucy muttered.

Judd wasn't sure if she'd want to know that such occurrences were quite common, so he tapped the horn lightly and waited for the lovers to vacate the road. Instead, they kept kissing as if they hadn't heard the blare of the horn. Judd tried again. No reaction.

He put the vehicle in park and stepped out, approaching the couple warily in case they mistook him for a willing third party.

"Excuse me."

They stopped kissing and looked at him as if he'd appeared out of nowhere.

"I need to get past, and I'm sure you'd be more comfortable on one of the ranch's many king-size beds," he said with a cheesy, customer-service smile, repeating the response Mason had taught him for any situation in which a couple was getting out of hand in public.

Without responding, the couple looked at one another and giggled, then crawled up off the road and wandered hand in hand toward the desert.

Judd climbed back into the Suburban and gave Lucy an apologetic grin. "I think they're about to give the coyotes an X-rated show."

Lucy's eyes widened for a moment. "Does this sort of thing happen often here?"

The wonder in her voice caught him off guard. "It isn't called Fantasy Ranch for nothing."

Before Judd could put the Suburban back into drive, he heard a nervous giggle only a few inches from his ear. He turned to find Lucy leaning toward him, her face next to his, and her bleary gaze focused on his mouth. She let out a little hiccup and Judd caught the scent of champagne and chocolate on her breath.

Her sudden nearness set his nerve endings on alert. "So I guess with all the crazy stuff that goes on here, you wouldn't be surprised if I did this."

And that was when she kissed him.

# 3

SHE WAS DOOMED before she even began. He tasted like manliness and fire and sin, and his lips—once he got past the initial shock of her planting one on him—were strong, the way she imagined a cowboy's lips would be. She felt herself melting, spinning, falling, sinking in—and it wasn't just the alcohol.

His five o'clock shadow created a friction on her upper lip and chin, and she could imagine that she still smelled the dust of the trail on him as she inhaled. She was finally kissing a cowboy. It was the best kiss she'd ever had.

Drunken bliss only lasted a few seconds, though.

He may have responded with his mouth, but he didn't touch her with his hands, and after a moment she got the vague feeling that she was behaving like a complete jerk. She pulled away. Averted her eyes. Stared intently at an air-conditioning vent. Her head swirled, but this time she feared it *was* the alcohol.

A merciful darkness descended.

When she came to, she had no idea how much time had elapsed, but it must not have been long because they'd only made it to the resort parking lot. And Judd must not have been too disturbed by her bad behavior because he was talking to her as if she were just another VIP guest. He was giving her an introductory tour, she guessed. She heard words like "facilities" and "Olympic-size pool" and "fifteen hot tubs," but her brain was too foggy to follow it all, so she simply wobbled dutifully behind him as he carried her bag along a stone path through the gates of the resort.

They passed cacti and other artfully arranged landscaping, faux rugged wood fences, low-slung Santa Fe-style stucco buildings. Here and there couples wandered through the warm desert night, and Lucy felt a pang of loneliness at being on vacation alone, tipsy from alcohol and having just made an inexcusable pass at her paid escort.

Through the champagne haze, she had one painfully coherent thought—tomorrow was her birthday.

JUDD SPRAWLED ACROSS the bed and eyeballed the cold beer just out of his reach on the nightstand. Nothing like handcuffing himself to a stranger's bed and impersonating the local Don Juan all night to make him too tired to lift an arm.

The recent memory of a certain champagne-induced kiss spurred him into action. He grabbed the beer and took a deep swig, trying hard not to think about how his body had responded so readily to Lucy's come-on. Somehow he had to keep his mind on the investigation.

Instead, memories of Lucy kept invading his head. Her lips coaxing him, her chocolate-flavored tongue tempting and teasing him... Damn it if he hadn't wanted to take her right there in the front seat of the Fantasy Ranch VIP vehicle.

And then there was her oddly awkward, utterly endearing reaction to the kiss. Her eyes the size of full moons, she'd sputtered and stammered an apology, expelled an hysterical string of giggles, and then passed out briefly. By the time Judd had gotten around to her side of the SUV to get her out, she was awake again, barely able to walk with him as he led her to her room. However much she looked like a party girl, she sure didn't handle her liquor like one.

The contrasts intrigued him. And her kiss had a tempting innocence about it that nearly drove him wild. *Stop it! Stop thinking about her.*

Judd cursed and dragged himself up off the bed and to the table where he kept his laptop and the files on his investigation—or lack of one. All he had was one sexy-as-hell suspect and no evidence to suggest her guilt, other than her employment at the travel agency.

He booted up the computer and opened the file entitled Sunny Horizons Employees. In it he'd listed all the agents who'd stayed at the Fantasy Ranch since the incidents of sabotage began. With the steep travel agent discounts they received, and the agency's proximity to the ranch, it wasn't necessarily unusual that five out of nine agents had visited there in the past three months.

He'd listed each one in order of the dates of their stay at the ranch, along with the lengths of stay and the instances of sabotage that occurred while each was there. It could have been coincidence, because acts of sabotage had been going on pretty steadily, sometimes while Sunny Horizons employees were present and sometimes when they weren't.

What he had was no evidence. He muttered another curse and took another swig of beer.

Only three of them, Frank Wiley, Rowena Kramer and Darren Ullrich, were there when more than one act of sabotage occurred. Maybe that meant something and maybe it didn't.

A hunch kept nagging at him. Mason's theory that this was all tied to Natasha Kendrick, his ex-girlfriend, was beginning to make more and more sense. It was just too convenient that she happened to be the CEO of Sunset Enterprises, and Sunny Horizons Travel was a direct subsidiary of Sunset. Were Lucy and her co-workers acting as Natasha's pawns? Were they getting paid to help ruin Mason's business?

Even that theory didn't explain all the instances of sabotage, though. There was still a big hole in the investigation.

He glared at the computer screen, willing it to produce some answers, willing himself not to think about one particularly cute suspect.

LUCY PREFERRED to sleep in flannel pajamas. In fact, she had a nice pair of gray plaid ones at home in her top dresser drawer. But last night she'd been forced to sleep in nothing but her cotton panties, because Claire had neglected to pack *any* sleepwear. Sure, there was that black lacy thing that looked more like a Victorian torture device than a woman's garment, but Lucy was quite sure it had not been designed to be slept in. And besides, she'd been a little too tipsy to work all the snaps and straps on the thing.

Apparently her friend didn't include pajamas on her list of life's little necessities.

As if that wasn't bad enough, Claire had filled the suitcase with items Lucy blushed just thinking about—thong underwear, lacy push-up bras, slinky dresses that left nothing to the imagination and, worst of all, a colossal box of condoms. It was just like that evil woman to embarrass Lucy with her warped sense of humor—and it did take a sense of humor to even suggest that Lucinda Jane Connors would ever need a hundred-pack of condoms for a one-week trip.

Lucy smiled at her friend's packing job in spite of herself. That was what she loved about Claire; they were such opposites. Although Claire was often infuriating, Lucy admired her and wished more than a little bit that she could be so outrageous.

This week was her chance. Her chance to find out what it would be like to ignore her every boring instinct—even do the opposite of what the nagging voice in her head automatically told her to do.

Now she had to force herself not to succumb to the urge to cover herself with the nearest napkin as she sat at the poolside bar in nothing but a shameful little black string bikini and a tight, sheer, black cover-up that covered up nothing at all. This, she reminded herself, is what the new Lucy would choose to wear. But the old Lucy missed her navy-blue one-piece with its low-cut hips and high-cut neckline. It might not have drawn stares from the opposite sex, but at least she could rest assured it would keep all the important parts covered when she took a dive into the pool.

Except, she wouldn't be diving into the pool with

the highlights she'd just had put in her hair this morning at the Fantasy Salon, and not with the forty-dollar makeup job she'd had done to conceal the effects of her hangover. It was her birthday today, and she'd treated herself. Aside from the obvious benefits, Lucy hoped her outward transformation would help provide the impetus for a more significant inner transformation. One not influenced by the effects of too much champagne.

Besides, until this morning, she hadn't had a clue about hair and makeup, but now she had a vague idea of what styles worked well with her face and what makeup colors went with her own natural coloring. Whether or not she'd be able to reproduce today's results was another matter entirely.

Xavier, the stylist and makeup artist, had spent two hours turning her into, in his words, "The woman she was meant to be." Lucy hadn't recognized the woman staring back at her when she'd looked into the mirror to examine Xavier's handiwork, but whomever it was had fabulous blond highlights and glossy pink lips that were a lot more voluptuous than Lucy's could possibly be.

She couldn't help wondering if Xavier's skill was what had been eliciting the stares of more than a few men since she'd taken her seat at the bar. It was either that or Claire's R-rated joke of a bikini.

She heard a commotion on the other side of the bar and looked over to see a gaggle of women surrounding one muscle-bound mountain of a man.

The bartender noticed her interest and leaned on

the bar near her to comment, "That's Buck Samson, you know."

*That* was the man Claire had intended to have handcuffed to her bed? Long, chestnut hair, a calendar-model face, a deep suntan, obscene muscle development, skintight T-shirt and jeans, he looked as though he'd just jumped off the stage of a strip club. She much preferred Judd's natural good looks, and if she'd found the real Buck in her bedroom, she might have actually passed out from the shock. And she definitely never would have agreed to come to the ranch.

The Buck Samson fan club—women of every size, shape and age—followed him to the pool and settled on chairs all around him. Lucy turned to stare, but found several men staring back at her instead of the spectacle created by Buck.

To avoid making contact with any of the resident lounge and pool lizards, she focused her eyes on her drink. But that left her to contemplate the way she'd embarrassed herself last night. She could only hope she wouldn't run into Judd today, even though part of her was dying to see him again. She could remember every detail of the night before with painful clarity, and the memories became clearer as the morning went on.

For heaven's sake, she'd kissed him! It was the most outrageous, uncharacteristic, stupid, irresponsible, utterly exciting thing she'd ever done. And now she had her whole birthday to spend regretting it. Well, maybe she didn't totally regret it, but she mostly did. After all, he hadn't exactly seen it coming, and while he'd behaved graciously under the circumstances, she could tell he'd been thrown off guard by the kiss.

But there had been sparks. It couldn't have just been the champagne talking, because she had seen in his eyes that he'd felt it, too. And he'd responded, answering her kiss with a little tentative exploration of his own. She'd been surprised by that, and a little empowered by it.

Mostly, she'd been blown away by it. The kiss, that is. Girls like Lucy didn't go around kissing guys like Judd, but she wanted to do it again. And again and again and again.

She'd emptied her virgin piña colada and was asking the bartender for another one when Judd appeared at her side, trapping her before she could escape.

"You slipped out early this morning. I've been looking for—" He stopped midsentence and gawked at her in a most disturbing manner.

Oh, no, her makeup was melting and turning her face into a bad Picasso. "What? What's wrong?"

"Nothing, it's just that you've changed."

She blushed under his scrutiny. "Oh, that. I found the salon brochure on my nightstand this morning and got an appointment."

"I didn't think you needed any beautifying." He continued to stare, taking in her hair, her makeup, her too-skimpy swimsuit.

Lucy felt her cheeks redden even more from the compliment and the scrutiny. "You didn't see the dark circles under my eyes this morning, or that lovely hangover glow I had."

He grinned. "Well, you look great."

She took a deep breath and turned to face him fully. "Judd, I need to apologize about last night. I never should have—"

"Don't say another word. We'll just pretend it never happened."

It was the same thing he'd said last night at the door of her hotel room as she'd apologized to him over and over again. But last night she'd been giggling throughout her string of apologies, and this morning she was serious. So was he. As far as she could tell, the kiss really hadn't bothered him.

Maybe that sort of thing happened to ranch employees all the time. The thought gave her a little queasy feeling, on top of the already queasy feeling she'd been dealing with all morning.

"Listen, I have some time off, and since today's your first day at the ranch, how about we go exploring?"

"Thanks, but you really don't need to keep me entertained," she said, unable to imagine why he'd want to spend the day with her after last night.

And then a thought occurred to her. Could it be that he was accepting her come-on, that he was interested? Her stomach did a flip-flop. Impossible...or was it? If her suspicions were correct, that meant Judd really could be the one!

He could be her wild fling, her one-night stand, the guy with whom she used a couple of those condoms Claire had packed for her. He certainly qualified, with his male-bimbo good looks, his unattached lifestyle on the ranch, and his seeming interest in her. And of course there were those sparks...

"Hey, I'm trying to keep myself entertained. So what do you say? Want to go explore?"

"I checked out the resort facilities on my own this morning."

"How about a little horseback riding then, or maybe some country line dancing lessons?"

Lucy could dance about as well as a three-legged cat.

"Horseback riding sounds great. I'll just need to change clothes."

"Hope you brought plenty of sunblock. You don't look like the type that tans easily," he said, scrutinizing her pale limbs.

"I'm wearing SPF 15, so I should be okay for a while." This was Lucy's idea of a big risk. She normally didn't go out in the sun with any less protection than SPF 45, a big hat and ideally, a nearby shade tree.

He gave her a doubtful look but didn't argue the matter, and she arranged to meet him at the stables in twenty minutes after she'd changed into something suitable for the outing.

Lucy raced back to her room, her mind a jumble of thoughts and her body a jumble of nerves. How could she keep up a conversation with her gorgeous bimbo companion for an entire afternoon? She was hardly known for her sparkling conversational skills. And how would she manage not to make a complete idiot of herself trying to hit on him? All her knowledge about seducing men could be summed up in one reading of *The Young Ladies' Guide to Dating*, a book her mother had given her for her sixteenth birthday, and whose old-fashioned tips Lucy hadn't even had the opportunity to try out until well into her college years.

She put on the one marginally practical outfit Claire had packed for her—a skimpy, fitted, white T-shirt, faded blue jeans and a pair of white sneakers. It wasn't exactly traditional riding gear, but it would have to do.

She found Judd waiting for her with both their horses saddled up outside the stables. After a cursory lesson from the stable hand on horse commands, they set off into the desert on a dusty trail the horses knew by heart.

Lucy did her best to guide her horse up next to Judd's after she'd been following behind him for a short while. Once she got within comfortable conversation distance, she scrambled to think of something to say.

"So do you ride often?" Lucy asked, images of a bare-chested Judd riding across the desert flashing in her sex-starved mind.

"Occasionally." He grinned. "Not often enough to know what the hell I'm doing."

He looked about as comfortable in the saddle as he might if he'd been riding a pink Huffy, but Lucy refrained from pointing that out. Maybe he was just having a bad day, or maybe he was uneasy around her after her bad behavior last night and his unease was affecting the horse, too.

Yes, that had to be it. She'd only been kidding herself to think that she could be a drunken fool for one night and get away with it.

No, no, no. She wasn't going to allow negative thoughts to ruin her day. Here she was, alone in the desert with a sexy hunk of a man, and Wild-and-Crazy Lucy was going to enjoy every minute of it she could.

She purposely changed the subject. "Tell me about your job. What do you enjoy about working here?"

"That would be the opportunity to spend the afternoon with a lovely lady like you," he said.

Even Lucy could recognize that as a line. False flattery probably came as naturally to a guy like him as breathing.

"You must meet a lot of women here."

Judd was silent for a moment. Then he said, "Oh, yeah, lots of ladies, and I love every one."

What more could she expect from a male bimbo? Lucy resolved not to let his comments bother her. On the contrary, she should feel good about them. He was the type of guy who *wanted* to be used for his body.

"How about you?" he asked. "Any men in your life?"

His interest caught her off guard, and she blurted, "No, I haven't dated for months."

Her face burned, and she slowed her horse in the hope of hiding her embarrassment from Judd. So much for her party girl image.

"Hey, babe, dating's overrated. You're like me, I bet—you like to stay footloose and fancy free, right?"

"Um, right." She was grateful for the out he'd given her, but she didn't feel like any less of a dork.

As they rode he asked her questions about her family, her hobbies and her interests, showing the attentiveness of a guy who was anything but an empty-headed bimbo. He'd listened so well and asked so many questions that she'd begun to feel interesting, even fascinating.

Judd was a gorgeous player who also knew how to listen? The contrast confused Lucy into silence after a while, as her conscience battled with her libido. She finally decided that he must have learned to be a good listener as part of his seduction game. He probably could bag more women that way—not that he needed help, with looks like his.

They'd been riding in silence for a short while when Judd turned and smiled at her. "What do you say we stop and give the horses a little break? I've got some sandwiches for us to snack on."

They found shade near some large boulders and sat on a blanket Judd spread on the ground. He leaned back and stretched his legs out, enjoying the break from the unfamiliar saddle.

It was scary how comfortable he felt around Lucy. Several times during their conversation, as she'd shared her history with him, he'd almost slipped and told the story of his police background, his investigation at the ranch, his failures with women. Hell, he'd even forgotten she was supposed to be his prime suspect.

Lucy unwrapped a sandwich and handed it to him, then began eating her own. She stared off into the distance, her wavy hair whipping in the occasional wind gust.

"What are you thinking about?" he asked, aware of how close he was coming to blowing his dumb

Fantasy Ranch image. But he didn't care. She fascinated him.

"Oh, just about a desert survival class I took in college, one of those bunny courses you take to fill up space between the hard classes."

Judd gritted his teeth as he saw his opportunity to turn himself back into a bimbo. "Yeah, college. I dropped out after the first semester. Drinking was more fun."

Lucy kindly ignored his dumb comment. "We learned all about how nothing is as it seems in the desert. Everything looks dead, dull, arid. But actually there's so much life just under the surface. There's a whole amazing, living world here if you look closely enough."

The passion in her voice surprised him. "You really like the desert, huh?"

She blushed. "I find it fascinating."

Fascinating, just like her. And full of contrasts. Was this the same woman who'd caught every guy's attention at the pool in her scandalous scrap of a swimsuit? For a sex kitten, she sure was deeper than she seemed on the surface. More alive and more vibrant than her party girl image implied.

Judd sensed that he was entering dangerous territory, a place where he could very easily get burned.

# 4

THANK GOODNESS it had been cloudy for their ride, or else her sunburn would have been even worse than it turned out to be. Her shoulders and arms were turning a little pink, she could see, even in the darkness of the Tex-Mex lounge where they were taking a break from the great outdoors. And her neck had the telltale burning sensation of skin that she'd forgotten to put sunblock on. After even that short time riding, she felt as if she had dust in all sorts of unseemly places, and her muscles were crying out from their unfamiliarity with the back of a horse.

As they sat across from each other in a booth, Garth Brooks played on the jukebox. When the waitress came, Judd ordered a Corona and a club sandwich, and Lucy ordered a virgin daiquiri and a basket of hot wings.

After the waitress left, Lucy couldn't think of another thing to say to this man she barely knew but had already set her mind on seducing. Instead of talking, she stared at the dance floor across the room, where a lone couple slow danced, indifferent to the mid-tempo music.

"Something on your mind?"

"Oh, no, just watching the lovebirds. I guess you see a lot of that around here."

He glanced over his shoulder. "Yeah, I hardly notice it anymore. Except when they're naked," he added with a little smile.

"I have to admit, I feel silly having you escort me around all day when we barely know each other."

"Hey, I know quite a bit about you. But let's get more acquainted. Tell me how you ended up in the travel agent business." His gray eyes sparked with unmistakable interest, and Lucy decided again that he was either a really good actor or a great listener.

The way he looked at her made her want to think of anything but her job, and her palms went all damp and clammy. He was too gorgeous for his own good.

The waitress came back with their drinks and Lucy took a sip before speaking. "I needed a change. I've only been in the business for less than a year, but I've always been interested because my best friend Claire runs the agency, and I envied her job. When I went through a little...upheaval last year, she invited me to come on board, so to speak."

"What sort of upheaval?"

Lucy's mouth went dry. She never should have mentioned that part of it. To this day she wasn't sure she could speak reasonably about the breakup. But then she looked at him again, and an image of that sexy razor stubble creating sweet friction on her cheek last night as she kissed him made her not care about getting dumped, for the moment.

"I was working as an accountant, engaged to one of my co-workers at the firm, and he dumped me."

"What sort of jerk would do that?" His eyes narrowed as he took a swig of beer and waited for her to explain.

"Well, to his credit, he probably did me a huge favor, but at the time it really hurt, and I needed a change of scenery. In fact, I didn't want to be an accountant at all anymore."

*At the time it really hurt?* That was the understatement of the year. Brad had dumped her for the forty-something office assistant whom he said was a more exciting woman to him than she could ever be. Lucy was happy to hear that a woman as prim and matronly as Barb had some hidden wild oats, but she certainly didn't want those oats being sown with her own fiancé. And Brad's comment didn't exactly soothe her ego.

Maybe Lucy was a boring lover. But that was the old Lucy—the one who believed sex was meaningless without love, the one who thought love could make up for lack of experience in the bedroom. Well, the new Lucy had wild oats to sow. She didn't have to wait for love, and she would get experience if that's what it took to interest a man. What better man to gain experience with than a shallow pinup boy like Judd?

Now it was just a matter of getting *him* to go along with her plans. She polished off a chicken wing with as much delicacy as the messy food would allow. Leaning forward, she licked the spicy buffalo sauce from her finger and asked, "Do you think I'm boring?"

He raised an eyebrow. "Is this a trick question?"

"No, it's just that my ex-fiancé left me because he said I was boring."

"He was a fool," Judd said without hesitation.

"You're just saying that." Lucy averted her eyes coyly, the way she'd seen Marilyn Monroe do in the movies.

He leaned forward and grasped her hand. "If you were boring, you wouldn't be here at the ranch. You'd be sitting at home clipping coupons for canned tuna or filing away your old magazines in chronological order."

"That's not so far off from what I had planned before you showed up handcuffed to my bed," Lucy blurted.

The statement had hardly left her mouth before she wished she could take it back. Her plans sounded a lot more pitiful out loud than they had in her head, and the momentary pity in Judd's eyes made her want to crawl under the table.

"Then you just didn't have the right company. No woman as pretty as you should be spending her birthday alone."

Lucy blushed at the flattery, suddenly unable to look Judd in the eye. Surely Judd was just going out of his way to be nice, but something about his simple compliment nagged at her.

A little punch struck Lucy in the chest. According to him, the flashy, made-up Lucy deserved his attention, but the boring old Lucy might just as well stay home and paint her toenails. She shouldn't have expected anything more substantial to come from the mouth of such a pretty-boy, but his comment still hurt.

What hurt even more was that she agreed with him. She'd gotten the boring life she deserved with her fear of risk-taking. Now that she was daring to live a little more on the wild side, she could see herself reaping the rewards that a nagging voice inside her told her she otherwise wouldn't have earned.

Squirming in her seat, Lucy mourned the loss of some small part of herself. For even if she could go back to her old life, she'd go with the knowledge of what it was like on the other side. She'd be forever changed, and whether that change would be positive, she didn't yet know.

JUDD STARED at the smooth slope of Lucy's neck, noting the sharp contrast along her collar between the skin that had been covered by her T-shirt and the skin that had not. She was beginning to show signs of sunburn.

"Um, did you forget to put sunblock on your neck?"

Lucy touched her neck and winced. "Yes."

"I should have said something when I saw you pull your hair up in that ponytail."

"No, it's not your fault."

"You should put something on that burn."

Their waitress appeared with drink refills. She set the two drinks down and frowned at Lucy's neck. "We keep aloe in the kitchen for burns. I'll bring some out to you."

She picked up their empty plates and left. A minute later she was back with a tube of aloe ointment, which she handed to Judd with a meaningful look. "You'd better take care of this lady of yours."

So there it was—his invitation to touch Lucy. It was

exactly what he wanted, and what he absolutely didn't want.

"You don't have to do that. I can put it on myself." She held out her hand, but Judd couldn't give up the tube.

"No, no. I'll do it." He stood and moved to her side of the booth, then slid in beside her. Their thighs touched briefly, and his groin came to life.

"Really, I can manage..."

Her voice faded as he squeezed some of the cool gel out and turned to her. Gently he rubbed the pink area between the collar of her T-shirt and her hairline. The heat from her body radiated out, heating first his fingers and then his entire body. In spite of the frigid air blowing from a nearby ceiling duct, Judd felt sweat break out on his upper lip.

"I never pass up the opportunity to rub lotion on a pretty lady," he said, feeling as cheesy as his statement.

Lucy studied him with her big brown eyes, for a moment looking unsure what to say. Then she looked away, a smile playing on her lips. "Too bad I didn't get my sunburn someplace more interesting."

That was the exact moment when Judd became sure he'd gotten in over his head.

"I QUIT."

Mason Walker looked up at Judd from a pile of paperwork and suppressed a yawn.

"I mean it. I can't spend another second with that woman." Judd paced across the room, glaring at Mason, who wasn't even making an effort to feign interest in his plight.

"Why not? She looks pretty hot to me. You should be thanking me, the way I see it."

"Thank you for making me dress up like a stripper? Thank you for giving me the world's lamest job?"

Someone knocked on the office door and before Mason could say "Come in," the door swung open. Filling the doorway was the six-foot-tall, Fantasy Ranch cowboy-on-steroids, Buck Samson. He propped one elbow on the door frame and struck a calendar pose, probably something he practiced at home in the mirror.

"What's up, Buck?" The lines of Mason's face took on the strained look that meant he was trying to control his temper.

Muscle Boy glanced at Judd. "We've got some business to discuss. In private."

"Seeing as how you're interrupting a meeting in progress, you'd better just tell me what you want right now."

"I saw those promo ads in the Phoenix paper. You said my name would be in really big print at the top of the ad."

Wow, he could read. Judd was almost impressed.

"Sorry, man. It didn't work out. And I never said at the top of the ad."

"My name isn't even *on* the ad!"

Mason sighed. "We may have accidentally left your name off."

Buck's eyes, a bright turquoise that could only have been from colored contact lens, narrowed to little slits.

"You'd better fix it. I'm gonna watch the paper all week, and if I don't see an ad with my name in big letters, I'm leaving this crap hole."

He shoved off the door frame and disappeared down the hallway.

Mason rolled his eyes, shook his head. "He threatens to leave about once a month. It's his way of asking for a raise."

"Why do you put up with it?"

"He draws a ton of guests. Women love him."

"You keep giving him raises?"

"Not as often as he'd like, but the truth is, his only other career option is to star in porn movies, and not even he wants to do that."

"Buck Samson has standards?" Judd made a mental note to check him out a little further.

"One or two, anyway." Mason glanced impatiently at his watch. "Aren't you supposed to be serving drinks at the Watering Hole pool right now?"

"No, because I quit."

"Oh, right. Then I guess you won't be interested in hearing the little tidbit about Ms. Connors I picked up on my own."

Judd wanted to feign disinterest, but the truth was that Lucy perplexed the hell out of him, and he was dying to discover all her secrets. And that was the problem. His wasn't a professional interest in her; it was a personal one. All the time he'd spent with her today, he could barely remember that he was supposed to be conducting an investigation, not having a great time with a beautiful woman.

He'd already ruined one career with his attraction

to women like Lucy, women who got under his skin and drove him crazy, women who made him toss aside common sense and do idiotic things such as sleep with the boss's woman. He'd sworn it would never happen again. He'd promised himself.

For several years now he'd been getting the urge to settle down, to get married, to start a family—but the women he met wanted none of that with him. He winced whenever he thought of his last girlfriend Carla's reaction when he'd told her their relationship had to either move forward or end. *Judd, honey, you're not the marrying kind. No woman wants to marry a guy like you, knowing every woman this side of the Mississippi's gonna want a piece of her man.*

As far as he could tell, he'd never really done anything to warrant the reputation of a heartbreaker, except maybe date a few too many women in his younger days. Women just assumed he couldn't be trusted in a long-term relationships because of his physical appearance.

He knew it was the reason Lucy had kissed him last night, and it was hard not to notice the way she stared at him as though he was a side of prime beef. His whole life, he'd let physical relationships like that satisfy him, since he couldn't seem to get anything better, but never again.

No, he wanted to find himself a nice woman, a woman who didn't care about appearances, maybe even a woman who was a little plain, since dating the gorgeous ones who understood their power over men had gotten him nowhere. He wanted a woman who wasn't going to make his blood boil. Someone he could have a slow, steady, reliable relationship with, one that would last.

Lucy definitely wasn't that someone.

"Are you gonna stand there glaring at me all day, or do you want to hear what I have on her?"

Against his own good sense he asked, "What?"

"I spotted her early this morning coming from the direction of the stock rooms, carrying a bag. I checked later, and a couple of the employee uniforms were missing. I know because we keep an inventory of them on the wall."

"So you think she's going to dress up as an employee for her next criminal act?"

"Exactly," Mason said, either ignoring or not noticing the sarcasm in Judd's response. "She took a bartender's uniform and a kitchen worker's uniform, so she could be planning to taint the food or drinks in some way."

"Wait a minute, aren't the stockrooms near the beauty salon?"

"Yes, why?"

"Lucy had her hair and makeup done there this morning. Maybe she was carrying a bag of hair products."

Mason frowned, obviously disappointed that his suspect had a possible alibi. "Hmm. She could have slipped into the stockroom on her way out of the salon."

"Or maybe she's involved in a sinister plot to dye everyone's hair red. The whole salon staff is in on it, providing her with—"

"Cut it out, smart aleck. Lucy's our only suspect at

the moment, with her connection to Sunset Enterprises."

It was a possible scenario, but Judd just couldn't picture Lucy doing something so underhanded. Even if her behavior was suspicious at times and her answers to his questions implied neither guilt nor innocence. Whatever secrets she was hiding, he hadn't gotten any sense so far that they were the scheming, devious kind. But he'd been fooled by beautiful women before.

His brother leaned back in his leather chair. "So what are you going to do with this information I've gotten for you?" He was obviously getting a little overexcited about his own detective work.

"Nothing. I told you, I'm quitting."

Mason shook his head. "I thought I could count on you, bro. Guess I was wrong."

"Yep, you sure were." Judd made a move for the door while he still could.

"You're attracted to her, aren't you? Afraid she'll break your heart like Carla did?"

Judd stopped in his tracks, cursing himself for ever revealing anything personal to his conniving brother. "You want to talk ex-girlfriends? How about psycho Natasha?"

"Natasha Kendrick is history."

"At least my 'history' doesn't try to burn down my house."

"Okay, you got me there. But don't you see, this is your chance to prove to yourself you can resist temptation. You keep an eye on Lucy for me, and at the same time, you benefit."

"I benefit?"

"You have to learn to live with temptation, man. This is your chance."

How had Mason managed to twist it all around like that? That was his skill, and he'd used it to his advantage all their lives. In fact, when he put it that way, Judd felt like a coward for quitting.

"I guess I could slip into her room when she's not there and look for the missing uniforms. That would at least give us some hard proof that she's involved in the sabotage," Judd said, realizing a moment too late that he was getting himself further involved in the investigation from hell.

Mason gave him a self-satisfied grin. "I knew you wouldn't let me down." He lifted a plastic key card from the desk. "I've got her room key for you right here."

JUDD PREFERRED not to resort to such underhanded tactics in his investigations, but curiosity won out where Lucy was concerned. He just couldn't resist getting a chance to sort through her stuff, to possibly find a clue that would help him understand why she behaved so strangely, as if she were putting on an act for his benefit.

Five minutes ago he'd watched from the hallway around the corner as she exited her room carrying a beach bag and wearing that unbelievable little scrap of a swimsuit, covered by some sort of see-through black gauzy thing that made his blood pressure instantly rise. She'd been humming the *Sesame Street* theme song, a detail completely incongruous with her sex-kitten image.

She was probably headed for the sunset beach party at the main pool, and he felt bad that she'd be spending her birthday evening alone while he snooped through her room. Women like Lucy never had to worry about being alone for long, though—a realization that gave Judd a misplaced pang of jealousy.

Now, inside the confines of her room, his conscience nagged him. How could he excuse snooping around a second time on a woman he admittedly liked so much? The first time, in her house, he really hadn't had much of a chance, since her friend had let him in and overseen his handcuffing to the headboard, but he'd still managed to take in quite a bit before he'd accidentally fallen asleep.

He'd formed a mental picture of Lucy based on her excessively neat home, her conservative furnishings, her seeming inability to decorate with any sort of daring. Judd might not have known much about interior design, but he knew enough to know that earth-tone-colored landscape prints didn't exactly indicate an adventurous personality. The only daring detail he'd noticed in her entire apartment were the sheets. They had been pale pink satin.

But he had to wonder, would a person with such conservative decorating tastes be the type to commit sabotage? He didn't know.

He stood in the middle of the room, his gaze stopping on each item that obviously belonged to Lucy and wasn't a permanent fixture. A pair of black high-heeled sandals, a curling iron, a gold tube of lipstick, a white sundress tossed onto the bed. The scent of shampoo lingered in the air and Judd's body responded as if Lucy herself was still in the room.

Fighting distraction, he tried to focus on business. This was his chance to learn something more about the woman who'd kept him awake half the night with lurid fantasies. This definitely wasn't the time for guilty feelings. His brother's business was in danger, he reminded himself as he crossed the room to the closet and opened the door to peer inside.

A few dresses hung from hangers, two pairs of equally frivolous but sexy sandals sat on the floor. He investigated the top shelf, the darkened corners, and the walls, but found nothing suspicious.

Against his better judgment, he went to the dresser and began systematically searching the drawers, knowing full well he was going to find the sort of skimpy undergarments that women as gorgeous as Lucy loved to tantalize men with. The top drawer yielded an array of lacy thong panties with matching bras, but he found no plans to blow up the Fantasy Ranch or to steal the ranch's secret barbecue sauce recipe. The next few drawers held bikinis, shorts, little summer tops—standard resort wear, but still nothing to indicate criminal activities.

As he pulled open the last drawer Judd gritted his teeth in an effort not to imagine Lucy in any of the frilly things he'd just seen. But the sole contents of the drawer sent his jaw sagging. He reached in and withdrew the biggest box of condoms he'd ever seen in his life.

Either Lucy's friend Claire was quite the practical

jokester, or Lucy was planning to set a new Fantasy Ranch record. He shook his head in amazement. At least she came prepared. As if his instincts hadn't been screaming loudly enough before to stay away from this woman, they'd now taken up a chorus inside his skull. He dropped the box back into the drawer and slammed it shut.

He scanned the room for further possible hiding places. Nothing stood out. He slid an open dresser drawer shut and glanced around to make sure nothing looked out of place, but that was when the door opened—almost silently, thanks to those newfangled card entry locks—and Lucy stepped inside and saw him.

A strangled sound escaped her throat, and her eyes widened in shock.

"Lucy, I was just—"

"Judd!"

His throat locked up. What had he planned to say? *Lucy, I was just searching your room for clues to your criminal activities.* Or maybe, *Lucy, I was just riffling through your underwear drawer.*

Neither, he suspected, would win him any points for good behavior.

"What are you doing here!" It came out as more of a screech than a question, her lovely peach complexion turning bright pink, and Judd felt himself thrust back into gear by her outrage.

"It was supposed to be a surprise," he blurted, hoping she wouldn't demand too many details, mentally kicking himself for not thinking of a cover story ahead of time. "A birthday surprise."

"What kind of birthday surprise?"

"It won't be a surprise if I tell you." *Tell her what? You idiot.*

Only one idea came to mind. One big stupid idea, fueled by visions of Lucy in a hot-pink thong and matching bra, and the flower scent of her girly shampoo lingering in the air.

"But I'm sure sneaking into guests' rooms isn't in your job description. Do you think your brother would approve?"

"Maybe not about the sneaking-in part," he improvised, "but he'd certainly approve of my intentions."

With that, Lucy's expression softened, and after an agonizing moment she let out an exasperated sigh. "Claire's behind this, isn't she? That woman can be infuriating when she wants to be. I'm sorry you got sucked into her little surprise."

Claire? Why hadn't he thought of that—some kind of surprise involving her friend. But now his one-track mind only focused on the one idea. One really bad idea he was quite sure would distract Lucy from his real intentions. And he couldn't very well say Claire was making him do it.

"Now that I know about Claire's surprise, why don't you just tell me what it is?"

"Actually, she has nothing to do with it. This is, um..." Was he really going to go through with it? He caught her scent one more time. Yes. Yes, he was. "This surprise is from me."

Her eyebrows perked. "What is it?"

"I can't tell you. It's something I just have to *do*."

Lucy stepped into his path, blocking the door with

all five feet seven inches of herself. "You're not going anywhere until you tell me what kind of surprise necessitated you breaking into my room."

She was more of a deterrent than a growling rottweiler in that moment. He stopped short. This was one damned stupid idea, but he couldn't think of any other way out.

He willed himself toward her. Lucy's eyes widened as she seemed to realize what her surprise might be.

"But...I don't understand why—"

She was frozen in place as he slid one hand around her firm little waist, and with the other, tilted her chin up toward him. He brought his mouth down over hers, effectively cutting off whatever logical protest she was about to make.

# 5

SOME WOMEN were made for kissing, and Lucy was one of them. Judd figured that out a moment too late. While his brain screamed for him to stop, his body had other plans. His lips, in particular, had no intention of listening to reason.

He deepened the kiss, ignoring the voice in his head. Lucy tasted like heaven, and she felt even better. His fingertips caught the soft skin at the back of her neck and lingered there, then traveled upward into the wild tangles of her hair. He wanted to get lost, to never have to think about why he shouldn't be kissing this woman.

Unlike their last kiss, this one wasn't prompted by alcohol, yet Lucy wasn't fighting it. At first she stiffened, but then the chemistry between them worked its magic and she was matching his fervor with her own, her arms snaking around his torso and hanging on for dear life.

He couldn't stop, he wouldn't stop...

The sound of fireworks punctuated their kiss. Fireworks, Judd mused. They were creating fireworks, there was so much explosive chemistry between them.

*Blam!*

*Kaplow!*

*Blam-blam-blam!*

And then he came to his senses. Fireworks! Those sounds were actual fireworks going off in the hallway outside Lucy's room. What the hell was going on? He pulled away and saw that her puzzled expression mirrored his own.

"Is that what I think it is?"

"It's not us then?" he asked, only half joking.

Lucy blushed. "Those sound like they're inside the building."

The commotion and rising voices in the hallway let them know they weren't the only ones who'd heard the explosions. Judd reluctantly released Lucy from his grasp and headed for the door, not sure whether he should feel alarmed or relieved that he'd been given the means to get out of her room without having to explain his uninvited presence.

A burning smell had already made its way under the door before he opened it. In the hallway, smoke obscured the faces of confused guests who'd milled out of their rooms to see what the commotion was.

This was another act of sabotage, Judd suspected, executed right under his nose as he fooled around with his primary suspect. Had this been planned? Had Lucy somehow known he was in her room and returned there to distract him while her partner or partners did no good? And if she was acting with someone, who could it be?

A man in a Batman suit stuck his head out of the room across the hall. "What's going on out here?"

From inside his room a woman's voice called,

"Come back to bed, Batboy!" The man shrugged and shut the door.

Lucy followed Judd out of her room. "I take it this isn't a normal occurrence at the ranch?"

The sound of a fire alarm pierced the air, and moments later the sprinkler system activated itself, sending hotel guests scattering in every direction.

"Not even on a busy week."

"Yikes."

"You'd better get out of the building, to be safe. I'll meet up with you later, once we've got this situation cleared up."

Still looking slightly dazed, Lucy nodded and followed the other guests making their way outside. Judd took a deep breath and shook his head in amazement that he'd managed to get out of that near disaster for the moment.

As he made his way through the water-and-smoke-filled halls, something was nagging at him. Something big.

And then it came to him. If Lucy was in her room kissing him, she couldn't have been involved in this pyrotechnics prank. That meant one of three things—either she wasn't involved in the sabotage at all, she was working with at least one other person or the fireworks weren't part of the sabotage plot.

He felt pretty confident in eliminating the last option, but what about the other two? Lucy appeared as genuinely shocked and confused by the sudden disruption of their kiss as he was. Now if only he could find someone carrying around fireworks and matches.

LUCY SAT AT A TABLE for two in the ranch's main restaurant, frowning at the empty seat across from her. It was the night of her twenty-ninth birthday and here she was having dinner alone, without even her cats to keep her company. Even worse, the sleaziest-looking guy at the bar seemed to have set his eye on her as his conquest for the evening. In his red silk shirt and skin-tight black pants, he reminded Lucy of everything that had been wrong with the seventies. His overgrown sideburns and mustache completed the picture of a fashion era gone wrong.

In the past half hour he'd had delivered to her table one scandalously-named mixed drink, one red rose and a pair of edible panties. Any place but the Fantasy Ranch, that last item would have been shocking, but here the guy carrying around the basket of roses also had a basket of undergarments in assorted flavors.

Lucy now possessed a pair of cherry ones.

She'd only eaten a few bites of her dinner and didn't have the heart to contemplate dessert. But then Judd appeared across the table from her, and she suddenly had in mind a dessert of an entirely different kind.

Ever since he'd kissed her—approximately two hours and fifty-four minutes ago—she could hardly focus on anything else. Her mind kept wandering back to the feel of his lips, the taste of him, the way that one little kiss made up for the previous twenty-nine years of her boring, risk-free life.

"You didn't think I'd let you spend your birthday night alone, did you?"

Lucy felt her face turn the same color as the cherry-flavored panties on the table. "I—I don't know."

"Sorry I couldn't catch up with you sooner. I

thought maybe you'd like some help moving to your new room. All the guests in your building are being relocated due to the smoke and water damage."

"I hadn't heard."

"I managed to get you relocated into a suite, seeing as how it's your birthday and all."

Now there was a luxury her salary usually couldn't afford her, even with travel agent discounts. "Wow, you shouldn't have, but I'm glad you did."

"After we get you moved maybe we could head on over to the pool party. I hear it's still going strong." He was referring to the very party Lucy had been headed to when she'd realized she'd forgotten her sunglasses and gone back to the room.

Lucy did a quick mental calculation of her dinner bill and then pulled out more than enough cash to cover it and the tip. She stood, dropped it onto the table and turned to leave, but as he rose, Judd nodded toward her gifts.

"Forgetting something?"

"Oh, gifts from my not-so-secret admirer." She surreptitiously nodded toward the guy at the bar.

"That guy in the red shirt?"

Lucy nodded. "Don't look straight over there!"

"What's that in the box?" he asked, peering down at the gift on the table.

"Edible underwear."

"Now that's the way to a woman's heart, don't you think?"

"I don't think it's my heart he's trying to gain access to."

He glared at the man in the red shirt for a moment longer than Lucy would have liked, but then again she sort of enjoyed his little show of protectiveness.

On the way back to her room, Judd explained how they didn't have any leads on who was responsible for the fireworks prank. It seemed to Lucy to be a bizarre thing to happen at a resort, especially one that didn't allow any guests under the age of eighteen.

"Why would someone set off fireworks in a hotel?"

"We think it's related to a string of problems that have happened over the past few months." He gave her an oddly speculative look. "Someone seems to be trying to ruin our business, or so I hear from my brother."

"But why?"

"I'm just the hired help. I don't get paid enough to wonder why."

Lucy peered at Judd sideways. Such a lame answer sounded false coming from him, even if he was a bit of a bimbo.

"Now that you mention it, I have heard a few negative reports lately about the ranch. I didn't connect them, though."

"What have you heard?"

Lucy strained to recall the stories passed around at the travel agency. "The food poisoning incidents two months back... Oh, and then there was the guest who complained of obscene phone calls to her hotel room. And wasn't there an incident recently where a bunch of reservations were lost from the computer system?"

"A year's worth."

"Anything else happen that I haven't heard about?"

"Some problems with theft, and some smaller incidents like customers finding strange things at their doors—strange even for this place."

"Like?"

"Gift-wrapped boxes filled with dog droppings, that sort of thing."

"That's awful. What makes your brother think these incidents are related?"

"They've been going on long enough and steadily enough, it's a fair assumption."

It seemed a little far-fetched to Lucy, but what did she know? They were at her hotel door now, and as she recalled all the embarrassing items she'd have to pack to vacate the room, she decided it would be best for Judd to leave.

"Thanks for walking me back to my room, but you really don't need to wait while I pack. Why don't you just point me in the direction of the suite and I'll meet you there in a half hour?"

"It's no problem. I'll just wait here so you don't have to haul that bag all the way across the ranch."

"There's no need—"

"Lucy, I insist. What kind of gentleman would I be if I made you move yourself?"

"It's only one bag." She felt her panic rising as she realized she wasn't getting out of this one... And besides, Wild-and-Crazy Lucy really did want to get Judd back into her room, maybe for a second round of what they'd begun a few hours earlier.

"One hefty bag, and one long walk to the Hacienda building."

Lucy sighed, wondering how she could distract him

from seeing the results of Claire's crazy packing job. And then she realized he might have already seen everything if he'd been nosy when he let himself into her room. Come to think of it, he hadn't appeared to have been waiting for her at all!

She forced her arousal-fogged memory to push past the very recent recollection of Judd's kiss to those confusing moments right before it happened. She'd unlocked the door, stepped inside, and there he was, standing in the middle of the room. His back had been partly to her and, if she remembered correctly, he'd been looking around. Not lounging on her bed the way she'd found him the first time. Not casually sitting in a chair waiting. Not behaving at all like a man prepared to give her a birthday surprise.

In his defense, maybe she'd caught him as soon as he'd walked in, and he hadn't yet found the perfect spot to wait for her. Yes, that had to be it. There was no other way to explain it. As she let her gaze linger for a moment on those heavenly lips of his, she knew she didn't want to get into a petty confrontation now over his entering her room without permission. It was Claire's fault for setting the precedent.

As she unlocked the door she turned to him and forced what she hoped was a nonchalant tone. "Let me just remind you that Claire did my packing and she has a really strange sense of humor."

"Remember, I work here. I've seen it all."

Lucy took a deep breath and stepped inside.

He followed her into the room and surveyed the water damage. "Looks like you just got a few wet outfits, huh?"

She picked up a damp dress from the bed. "Guess I won't be wearing this tonight."

"The ranch will take care of any dry cleaning you have because of the smoke or the sprinkler system. Just leave a note with it for the laundry service."

"No big deal. Seems like the most appropriate attire at every event here is a string bikini."

"Is there anything I can help with?"

She had to distract him long enough to at least get the most embarrassing items hidden in her suitcase. "How about you clear my things out of the bathroom, if you don't mind?"

He disappeared into the bathroom and Lucy rushed to the dresser. She flung open drawers and grabbed all the most potentially mortifying things she could find. She'd only made it halfway across the room to her suitcase with the armload of stuff when Judd reappeared.

"Do you have a bag for all this?" His gaze dropped to the load in her arms, lingering for an extra moment on the king-size box of condoms.

Lucy's face burned. "It's under the sink."

A wicked grin played across his lips. "Planned a busy vacation, eh?"

"It was Claire. I told you—the woman I'm going to murder the next time I see her."

"I know, I know. Couldn't resist."

She balled up a black satin push-up bra in her fist and threw it at his head, but he ducked. The bra landed on the bed behind him as if it had been artfully arranged there for a lingerie ad. They both stared at the bra, then at one another. If she weren't mistaken, she saw unbridled desire in his eyes.

"Your friend has pretty good taste."

"Sometimes. However she also picked out these." Lucy held up a pair of sheer red panties covered in rhinestones and tiny boa feathers.

One eyebrow perked up, and he suppressed a grin. "Not your style?"

"I try to avoid bejeweled underpants."

"Yeah, me, too."

Lucy dumped the armload of lingerie and condoms into her suitcase, no longer so embarrassed by them. She emptied the rest of her drawers and the closet the same way without bothering with folding. All her natural instincts were screaming at her to take everything back out and fold it neatly, then rearrange it by category inside the suitcase.

Judd peered into the overstuffed suitcase. "Nice packing job."

Lucy slammed it shut and sat on top to make zipping it possible. Once she'd gotten that done, she gave the room one last quick survey before they took off.

By the time they made it to the Hacienda building where Lucy's new room was located, she was glad Judd had come along to carry the suitcase. The long walk across the resort in her ridiculous little sandals left her feet aching, and the heat of the day hadn't yet worn off, even though the sun had set.

Judd escorted her into an elevator, then down a cool, dimly lit hallway to the room at the very end. Inside, he hit the light switch, revealing the most outrageously decorated hotel suite Lucy had ever laid eyes on. Ruggedness and luxury were combined and taken to the extreme. It looked vaguely familiar from a Fantasy Ranch brochure she'd once browsed, but seeing it in person had a much greater impact.

Her gaze focused immediately on the gigantic bed, with its huge, rustic headboard and footboard, masked by mosquito netting that hung from the ceiling. Above it, not surprisingly, were mirrored panels set in a tray ceiling. Oversize sage velvet armchairs and ottomans contrasted with rugged wood tables and details.

Lucy set foot in the bathroom and her jaw sagged. Accented by Southwestern-motif tiles and a saguaro cactus in the corner was the biggest jetted bathtub she'd ever seen. She could throw a party Fantasy Ranch-style in the thing. Recessed lighting gave the huge bathroom a calm, classy feel. When she spotted the oversize shower with the dual showerheads, her imagination took hold and she had to push aside images of her and Judd, drenched in water—

"Nice bathroom, huh?"

"Yeah, nice." Beads of perspiration formed between her breasts, and she hoped her blush didn't make what she'd just been thinking too obvious.

"Did you see the balcony yet?"

When she shook her head, Judd motioned for her to follow him. While her previous room had a small balcony just big enough for a bistro table and two chairs, this one had a balcony big enough for entertaining. Two deeply padded chaise longues plus a table and chairs still left room for a little slow dancing or whatever else anyone might want to do on their own private balcony at midnight. They stood for a moment looking out over the moonlit desert, until the distant sound of music and a boisterous whoop pierced the quiet.

"Sounds like the pool party's still going strong. Want to check it out?"

Lucy took note of his body language—arms crossed, shoulders stiff, body half turned away—and decided maybe he was just being polite after all. They'd been alone in both her rooms for more than a half hour and he hadn't so much as looked at her cross-eyed, let alone behaved flirtatiously.

Maybe that kiss hadn't been what he'd hoped. Maybe she had doggy breath. Maybe he thought she really had packed that box of condoms herself.

"Come on now, you're not gonna back out on me, are you?"

"Well..."

"It's your birthday. You owe me at least one dance." He smiled and tugged at her hand, pulling her toward the door.

Maybe his standoffishness was just her imagination, after all.

"I owe you a dance?"

"Repayment for lugging your suitcase all this way."

"You volunteered!"

"I had my reasons."

She felt herself melting, turning to butter in his hands. When he put it that way, dancing the night away with Judd didn't sound like a bad idea at all, even if she didn't know how to dance.

FANTASY RANCH PARTIES were legendary among resort-goers. Judd had never attended one himself, but he'd heard things.

Tonight's sunset pool party had been going strong for hours by the time he and Lucy arrived. The theme was Leather and Lace, and apparently everything in between, judging by the variety of attire. A woman wearing nothing but pink cling wrap jiggled past them, followed by a guy in black leather chaps and matching bikini briefs.

Ahead of him, Lucy stared for a moment too long at a guy wearing a Zorro-style mask and cape, and he mistook her for an interested admirer.

"You like dance?" he asked in a heavy Russian accent.

"No, thank you," she sputtered, sidestepping his outstretched hand.

Judd made sure to walk closer to her the rest of the way around the pool, making her less an object of interest to the many single men in attendance.

She stopped in her tracks before Judd noticed, and he walked right into her. His hands went immediately to her waist to catch her from tumbling forward. They lingered there for a moment, and he wondered how he was going to make it through the night without taking her to his bed, let alone make it through an entire week.

Yet he'd walked right into this situation. He could have bowed out for the night. He could have made any number of excuses. Instead, he'd felt bad for her spending her birthday night alone, and he told himself he was sticking around her for the sake of his investigation. He'd lied.

No one had seen anything strange related to the fireworks incident. He wasn't any closer to finding a saboteur now than he had been a week ago when Mason hired him.

They found a table that had just been vacated by a group of middle-aged women in lacy negligees. Across from him, Lucy surveyed the wild crowd with wide eyes. Maybe he should have warned her. The Fantasy Ranch by day was a grown-up-fun kind of place, but by night it was downright swinging, especially in the eyes of anyone who lived a marginally sheltered life. He hadn't suspected that about Lucy. Women who looked and dressed as she did usually knew the score, but he could tell by her expression that she was far less jaded than he'd given her credit for.

Again, she'd managed to surprise him. Was her whole sex-kitten image just an act? And if so, what did she hope to accomplish with it? If her goal was to drive him wild, she was succeeding. But something told him there was more to her story than that.

The investigator in him was just dying to uncover the truth about Lucy's contradictions; the man in him was defenseless against her good girl/bad girl charms.

The music was too loud to allow for conversation, he realized, so once the waitress had taken their drink orders and brought them out, he invited Lucy to dance.

She gave him a reluctant look.

"Remember, you owe me."

"I'm an awful dancer."

"You can't be any worse than me."

"I'd rather you not find out just how bad I am."

He tugged at her hand, but she remained planted in

her seat. Judd hadn't expected this from her, either.
Wild party girls usually loved to dance.

"Okay, take a look at the people dancing."

Lucy peered out at the gyrating crowd, most of
whom were hopelessly rhythm-challenged, seriously
drunk, nearly naked or a combination of the three,
and she cracked a half smile.

"Even if you're the world's worst dancer, no one
will notice. Now come on, birthday girl."

This time she let him pull her up, and he led her
onto the makeshift dance floor just in time for a slow
song. His sensible side had hoped for them to maintain a little distance, but his not-so-sensible side—the
one that always got him into trouble—said a silent
prayer of thanks for the good timing.

After she smashed a couple of his toes, Lucy settled
into his arms and let him lead. With couples engaged
in hip grinding of every imaginable variation all
around them, they had little room to move, so Judd
stayed in place and swayed with her to the music, trying his best to ignore the overwhelming urge he had to
kiss her again and to find out if all that chemistry he'd
felt earlier had been real or imagined. She felt so good
in his arms, as though she was meant to be there. The
temptation was almost too much.

He wouldn't kiss her again, though. Absolutely not.
Out of the question... But if she happened to kiss him?
Well, he couldn't be responsible for what happened
then.

# 6

A SHRILL RINGING lured Lucy out of her dream involving Judd and a bubbling hot tub full of chocolate sauce. *Oh, no, more fireworks. They'd set off the fire alarm again. No, just the phone. Better answer it, could be Mom calling to ask why you haven't given her any grandchildren yet.* "Hullo?"

"So have you bagged any hunks yet?"

Lucy tried to focus her eyes on the digital clock on the nightstand. It couldn't possibly have been correct. She never slept until noon!

"Hey, Luc, you still there?"

"Yes, I'm here," she croaked in her rusty morning voice. "Claire?"

"I woke you up, didn't I!" She let out a delighted squeal. "It's about time you stayed in bed past six o'clock. I knew the Fantasy Ranch would do you good. Now just tell me there's a naked hottie in bed next to you and you'll have made my day."

"Sorry to disappoint."

"But what about Buck? Not your type?"

"Claire, I've only been here two nights! And there is no Buck, or at least he's not the guy that accompanied me to the ranch."

"But I met him at your apartment to let him in—"

"No, you met Judd Walker. Don't worry about it,

long story." Lucy pushed herself up in bed and pulled the covers up to hide the scandalous little white teddy she'd dared to sleep in last night.

"So did you bag *him?*"

"There hasn't been any bagging going on, period. At least not in my room—yet," she couldn't help adding as she remembered Judd's kiss from the day before, and the way he'd held her as they'd danced last night. And the way her entire body had turned into a pulsing, throbbing bundle of nerves while pressed against him.

"O-oh, I love the sound of that! Details, please."

"Yesterday I came back to my room to get my sunglasses, and he was waiting for me there." Lucy paused, breathless. "He kissed me and it was... heavenly."

On the other end of the line she heard only silence for a moment. "That's all?"

"What do you mean, 'that's all'? Isn't that enough?"

"It's a start, I suppose."

"Okay, we also went out dancing last night."

"You didn't bag him after that, either?"

Lucy sighed, remembering how wonderful it felt for once in her life to just dance, not worrying one bit about how silly she looked or how little rhythm she had. In Judd's arms—and later when she'd worked up the courage to fast dance with him—she had even felt like a pretty good dancer.

"He was a perfect gentleman all night."

"Oh, one of *those* guys," Claire said as if she'd just found out he wore argyle socks to bed.

"Maybe he's letting me set the pace."

"It sounds like you need some help letting your hair down, girlfriend. I'll be there this afternoon."

Lucy sat up a little straighter. "What about your conference?"

"I'm leaving early, and besides, how can I resist witnessing my favorite wallflower's coming out week?"

"This place isn't nearly as interesting as it sounds."

"I'll be there by five o'clock."

And then Lucy heard a click. She stared at the receiver for a moment before returning it to the nightstand, not exactly shocked that Claire had hung up on her again to avoid an argument.

At least she would have someone to hang out with. She couldn't feel too annoyed with Claire, not when her presence always promised fun.

Lucy hopped out of bed and headed for the shower, but paused in front of the full-length mirror as she passed it. Was that really her casually strolling across the room in a teddy? The few times she'd worn one of these things in the past for an old boyfriend, she'd felt the need to scoot across the room sideways using her pillow as a barrier.

Now here she was walking around as if she felt at home in the transparent lacy thing. For a few moments she'd actually forgotten her nearly naked state. Amazing.

After showering and dressing, she decided she'd go out and find Judd herself, perhaps even let him know that she was ready to continue where they'd left off if he was willing. A little heat wave swept through her at that thought.

It was the first day of a brand-new year for Lucy,

and somehow, some way, she was going to start it out right by bagging herself a man. But not just any man. She would settle for no less than Judd Walker.

IF THERE WAS ONE THING Judd hated more than serving drinks to the guests lounging around the pool, it was serving drinks to the guests lounging around the pool while wearing the world's stupidest cowboy getup. No real cowboy in the history of the West had ever worn a white Stetson, a bolo tie with no shirt, a pair of cutoff faded-denim shorts and white cowboy boots. And whoever had invented cowboy boots obviously hadn't intended them to be worn by cocktail waiters.

Judd and most of the other waiters agreed that they looked more like male bunnies at some sort of gay Playboy mansion than anything a heterosexual woman would want to ogle, but nonetheless, the female guests loved the outfits. In fact, the waiters were a legend among resort-goers, and it was rumored that scoring with one of the Fantasy Ranch staff was a coveted souvenir for the wilder guests.

Speaking of wilder guests, his very favorite one had just appeared minutes ago on the other side of the pool. He couldn't help staring at her whenever he got the chance as she sat in a lounge chair, reading a thick paperback novel and wearing the sexiest little scraps of hot pink fabric he'd ever seen. Other guys noticed, too. The various single men at the pool took their turns staring, but Lucy seemed oblivious.

She might have started out dancing like an inhibited little wallflower last night, but by the third song, she was swinging and gyrating like a wild party girl, and half the men at the party were eyeing her with unbridled interest. By the end of the party, it took every ounce of his willpower not to spend the rest of the night finding out what other moves she knew, but he'd managed to resist. And she had turned oddly shy as he'd walked her back to her room, not even offering a good-night hug, let alone a kiss.

Lucy was a fascinating bundle of contrasts, a mystery the investigator in him couldn't wait to solve. On the one hand she exuded raw sex appeal and looked like a party girl, but she didn't act the part. The more time he spent with her, the more he began to wonder if one of her sides was just an act.

"Oh, waiter!" someone behind him called, and he realized the frozen daiquiri he was carrying was in danger of totally melting in the desert sun if he didn't hurry up and serve it.

Judd set the drink on the small table next to the woman who'd called for him. Nearly blinding him with her shiny gold swimsuit, she smiled and tucked a bill into the waistband of his shorts. He hated the guests touching him in such a familiar way, but Mason had instructed him to endure it unless things got out of hand.

Forcing a smile, he asked if she needed anything else and then headed back to the bar to pick up his next order. On his way he cursed his brother for what must have been the hundredth time for turning him into a faux male bimbo. When he'd left the police force to open his private investigation business, he'd never once envisioned himself serving girly drinks and getting bills tucked into his cutoffs.

Maybe the humiliation was his punishment for sleeping with the boss's woman, or for past indiscretions in general.

"This one's for the babe in the pink bikini in chair eighteen." The bartender motioned in Lucy's direction. "The guy on the other side of the bar sporting the Speedo from hell is sending it. Wants you to tell her it's from her secret admirer."

It was the same guy that had been ogling her in the restaurant yesterday. "What's the drink?"

"Sex on the Beach, of course." The bartender rolled his eyes and turned to another customer.

That particular drink was a popular one here at the ranch for single men ordering drinks for women. It ran a close second to the Screaming Orgasm. Judd couldn't imagine sending such a drink to a woman he wanted to impress, but then, he wouldn't choose to vacation at the Fantasy Ranch, either.

As he walked around the edge of the pool toward Lucy, with her drink and several others balanced on a tray, two women murmured appreciative "oh baby"-type comments as they inspected him from head to toe. He thought he would have gotten used to such scrutiny by now, but instead he was feeling more and more like a slab of meat hanging in the butcher shop. He'd always tried not to rely on his looks for anything in life, and he'd never been the type to dress in skin-tight cutoffs.

"You've got a couple of fans." Lucy lowered her sunglasses and nodded her head toward the women he'd just passed.

"I know, so do you." He set the drink on the table. "Sex on the Beach, from Speedo Man at the bar."

"Another one?" She sat up in her chair and glared across the pool at her admirer. "That guy won't leave me alone!"

"Has he been bothering you again?"

"Yes, well, not exactly. He keeps sending me drinks, and he won't stop staring over here, and he had this bottle of suntan oil delivered to me with a little message attached." Lucy nodded to an hourglass-shaped brown bottle.

Judd picked it up and read the label. "'Heavenly Bodies Tanning Oil.'" He then looked at the small card attached. "'A gift with a thousand creative uses. Love, Your Secret Admirer.'"

"Charming, huh?"

He felt a surge of protectiveness for Lucy, as if she were his...girlfriend. Ridiculous. He tried to ignore the Neanderthal urge to pound on Speedo Man. "Want me to tell him to go jump off a cliff for you?"

"I'd feel like a jerk ruining his day just because he wants to flirt."

Judd peered across the pool at him. "That guy looks pretty slimy to me. How about we get out of here so you don't have to put up with him?"

"No, I'm fine, and I don't want to interrupt your work."

The woman in the gold swimsuit passed by and gave Judd a pat on the rear end.

"This place is a meat market," Lucy said.

He smirked at their parallel thoughts. "You're telling me."

She raised one eyebrow. "I take it you're not all that satisfied with your job."

He sat the tray down on the table and sank into the chair next to her. "If by 'not satisfied' you mean ready to bust out of this joint, I guess I'm not."

"But the money's good, right? Probably even better than you could earn as a stripper or a...a gigolo."

She was making a joke with those suggestions, but she obviously did think he was skilled for nothing but displaying his body to the public. He knew he shouldn't have used Mason's suggested cover story for his job history.

"Very funny."

"Sorry." She took a sip of her drink and relaxed into her chair a bit more, her back doing a little arching maneuver that nearly got him hard right there, poolside. There definitely wasn't any room for an erection in these shorts.

"You're forgiven."

"Have you ever thought of male modeling? I mean, you obviously have the look. I bet you're pretty photogenic."

He bit his tongue. Damn it if she wasn't giving him career advice based on his fictional repertoire of male bimbo skills.

"I think I'll pass on being a coverboy." Judd glanced down at the tanning oil and remembered Lucy's sunburn. "How's your neck?"

"Oh, fine. Just a little tender. Don't worry, I'm covered from head to toe in SPF 40 today."

"Smart lady."

"Don't you still have to serve those drinks?" She

nodded to the two whiskey sours that were now watered down because the ice in them had melted.

Great, he was a lousy waiter, too. "Guess I'd better get right on that."

The two elderly men on the other side of the pool waiting for their drinks were glaring at him and gesturing angrily. No tip from them, he guessed as he walked away from Lucy, trying to ignore the giant blisters on his feet. Judd decided right then that he couldn't spend another minute playing Bimbo Waiter.

He stopped in his tracks. "Seriously, how about we blow off this scene?"

Lucy eyed him suspiciously. "Don't you have to work?"

"I'm getting blisters on top of my blisters in these damned boots. I've had enough of this waiter gig."

"I don't want to be responsible for you losing your job."

Judd cursed himself silently for what he was about to say, since it would only reinforce his loser image. "Don't worry babe, my brother's the boss. I can skip work when I need to. Besides, Speedo Man over there looks like he's about to make his move on you."

She grimaced.

"I could give you a backstage tour of the resort. Interested?"

"Sure, why not," she said as she put on her cover-up.

He wasn't sure exactly what he hoped to learn on their tour, but he figured some opportunity would have to arise for him to test her involvement in the sabotage, to see just how much she already knew about the resort.

As they left the pool area, heading for the employees-only section of the main hotel, an angry-looking man stopped Judd.

"Hey, you work here, right?" The man nodded to indicate Judd's bimbo suit.

"Gee, what makes you think that?"

"Look here, smart aleck. I've got a notion to sue this place after what my girlfriend just found." He held up a condom, still in its black foil wrapper. "See this?"

In the center of the condom packet was a perfectly round hole. Judd could see the tip of the man's nose through it.

"Looks like you've got a faulty one there."

"This is from the hotel's complimentary condom basket. We took ten of them, and they're all like this!"

"Planning for a busy night, huh?"

The man didn't seem to appreciate his joke.

Lucy took the packet from him and peered closely at it. "It almost looks like someone took a hole puncher to it. You know, one of those little handheld office devices?"

"This is grounds for a lawsuit, I tell you! Do you realize what could have happened if I hadn't noticed the hole ahead of time?"

Judd bit his lip, trying not to laugh. "Yes, sir. If you could just give me your name and room number, I'll be happy to call the problem to the attention of my manager and make sure he gets in touch with you right away."

The irate guest seemed temporarily appeased. "If I

don't here from him today, I'm calling my attorney," he called over his shoulder as he stormed away.

"I can see the headline now. 'Hedonistic Resort Promotes Unsafe Sex With Holey Condoms.'"

"Who would do such a thing? That's a really awful prank, considering the potential consequences."

The saboteur had struck again. Judd studied Lucy closely, looking for any sign that she was pretending to be surprised by the prank. She looked genuine enough.

He escorted her on to Mason's office, where he introduced Lucy to Mason and let his brother know about the condom prank—and the fact that he was skipping work at the pool to give Lucy her "tour." Mason flashed Judd a questioning look, but shrugged in agreement as he walked out of his office to deal with the angry guest.

Lucy stopped by a bulletin board full of photos taken at the ranch. Various pictures of guests, parties, events and employees filled the board. She studied it, smiling at some of the more outrageous shots, and then her gaze stopped on one that was hardly visible, half covered by other photos. It was of Buck Samson engaged in a discussion with someone Judd didn't recognize.

"Hey, I know him! We work together."

A little alarm bell sounded in Judd's head. "You work with that guy talking to Buck Samson?"

"Yeah, it's Frank Wiley, one of the agents at Sunny Horizons. I remember him visiting here a few months back." She frowned. "What on earth could he and Buck have had to talk about?"

What, indeed? Judd carefully kept his expression neutral, and Lucy shrugged and turned away from the photographs. Not exactly the reaction of a guilty party.

"This—" Judd motioned down the hallway, his hand accidentally brushing Lucy's shoulder "—is where all the administration takes place."

For such an innocent touch, it sure managed to send shock waves through him. Judd quickly dropped his hand to his side.

"Neat," Lucy said as she surveyed the administration area.

She actually was looking interested in hearing about how the ranch was run, but Judd's mind was still racing over her reaction to the photograph. If she were involved, no way would she have pointed out that picture.

He was almost sure, he realized suddenly, that she had nothing to do with the sabotage.

His enthusiasm for playing fake tour guide died instantly, but seeing her obvious interest in all the boring details of running a resort, he couldn't help but continue on their tour. He realized, too late, though, that he couldn't be a very interesting guide, given his limited knowledge about all the workings of the resort, but Lucy didn't seem to mind.

Outside in one of the cactus gardens, Lucy pointed out a pond with a statue of two reclining lovers in the middle of it. "What's the story behind that statue?"

Hmm. He should have admitted that he didn't know, but instead he opened his mouth. "This is

Lover's Pond, and that's a monument to the two lovers who died here in a freak hot-tub accident."

Her eyes widened. "Really?"

A ridiculous story took shape in Judd's head, and he managed to keep a straight face. "The state of Arizona considered banning hot tubs because of what happened here."

"Wow, I never even heard about it. What did happen?"

"This couple sneaked into one of the public outdoor hot tubs late at night, after it was closed, and they turned it on. But they didn't know how to adjust the temperatures properly, and pretty soon they started feeling uncomfortably hot. Really, really hot."

"Oh, no."

"Before they knew what was happening to them, they'd been—" he paused for dramatic effect "—*boiled alive.*"

Lucy stared at him, incredulous for a moment before the truth dawned on her. Then she smiled and gave him a playful swat on the chest. "You liar!"

There it was again—the bolt of electricity that shot through him at the slightest physical contact with her. She must have felt it, too, because she jerked her hand back and blushed.

"Sorry, I shouldn't have hit you like that."

Judd feigned receiving a blow to the chest. "Oh, you knocked the air out of me." He put his hands on his thighs and leaned over, pretending to gasp for air. "You'd better watch out, you don't know your own strength."

Lucy puffed up her chest a bit. "Yeah, I was on the wrestling team in high school."

"*You?*" He eyed her slight figure, trying to imagine her pinning some hulking athlete to the mat.

"I won state my senior year, beat a girl twice my size."

Judd laughed. Now he was the one being had. "Okay, you had me going there for a minute."

This was bad, bad, bad. Not only was Lucy an irresistible combination of naughty-and-nice girl, but he enjoyed talking to her, too.

From the pond they made their way along a path to the main restaurant. They entered from the front and Judd led her back to the kitchen.

"Um, I haven't worked in here before, so I can't tell you much," he said over the swishing of a giant silver dishwasher.

Lucy glanced around. "I worked in a kitchen one summer during college. It was the sweatiest, greasiest job on earth."

The tall, lanky cook standing at the grill looked up and glared at Lucy. She smiled and waved.

An image of Lucy drenched in sweat and oil, wearing a bikini, appeared in Judd's head, and he immediately banished it.

She motioned to the area nearest them. "This is where the finishing touches are put on the food before it goes out—garnish, toppings, things like that."

Judd nodded, watching as she picked up a bottle of spray whipped cream and shook it.

Lucy flashed a smile. "You look like you could use a cream shooter."

"A what?"

"Close your eyes and open your mouth."

Judd reluctantly obeyed, and a moment later he heard the sound of the aerosol can and felt his mouth filling up with whipped cream. She didn't stop until he closed his mouth.

"Oops, I got a little on your lip." She reached up and dragged her finger along his lower lip slowly, then brought the excess whipped cream to her own mouth, and with her gaze locked on him, tentatively licked her finger clean.

It was a blatant sexual invitation, one Judd got the odd feeling she didn't make often.

"Hey, you two!" the cook yelled. "Do you want me to tell you all the health codes you're violatin' right now?"

"We're leaving, we're leaving." Judd took Lucy's hand and tugged her out the door.

For the remainder of their tour, he pretended he knew what he was talking about—most of the time sounding like an idiot—while Lucy ignored his embarrassing lack of knowledge.

In fact, she humored him a little too much, making comments like, "Oh, you can't be expected to remember such things," when he fumbled over a detail. Clearly she believed he was an empty-headed bimbo, and she was too nice to say it outright. His pride screamed at him to prove that he was an intelligent person, but he couldn't blow his cover now.

By the end of their tour, Lucy had ceased asking questions, probably having come to expect that he'd be too dumb to know the answer anyway. And Judd had given up trying to catch her in a lie. She just seemed too genuine a person, too earnest in everything she said and did, to be deceiving him. Either that or she was a really good actress.

Maybe it was time for him to stop acting like such a dimwit. At least then he wouldn't feel so embarrassed to be around her.

"Feel like watching the performers practice for the Wild West Show?"

"Sure, that sounds great."

He led her to the theater, where the stage was filled with dancers practicing. The Fantasy Ranch's version of a Wild West Show was hardly like any other. It was a sort of cabaret meets the Old West, historical accuracy be damned.

They found seats in the darkened theater, while up on stage a parade of scantily dressed bar girls sang about offering drinks and other pleasures to the cowboys who lounged around at scattered bar tables, themselves wearing little more than their cowboy hats.

"We got lucky. It's a dress rehearsal."

"Will they mind us being here?"

"Staff are always welcome to watch and offer feedback on the show," Judd improvised, not aware of any such policy. He just wanted a chance to sit here with Lucy for a while. For the investigation officially, but unofficially because he craved her company.

On stage, the bar girls had all chosen cowboy partners and were now doing scandalous dance moves on their laps.

"Oh, my. Do they really do this in front of an audience?"

"Yep."

He glanced over and caught Lucy blushing. *Blushing?* She never stopped amazing him with her incongruities. One minute he felt as if he'd better protect himself from her dangerous charms and the next he was sure he needed to protect her from the big jaded world out there.

A transformation came over her. She gave him a sultry smile and slid her hand into his. "I like it."

The physical contact made Judd's body respond like a schoolboy's. He shifted uncomfortably in his seat, all too aware that his ridiculous denim cutoffs left no room for schoolboy responses. If Lucy simply touching his hand had this effect on him, he could only begin to imagine what more serious contact would do to him. He'd be a lost man. Out of control. Crazed. He'd be stupid to let this go too far.

And that was exactly what he wanted to do.

As they watched the rehearsal, Lucy's hand moved slowly from his knee upward, hesitating, then sliding up a little more. If he hadn't been so damned turned on, he would have laughed at how her strange awkwardness reminded him of his own adolescent attempts to feel up a girl in a theater for the first time.

By the time the bar girls of the Old West had conquered their cowboys and wrangled them into marriage, Lucy's tentative little hand had made it to ground zero. He glanced over at her to see that she was again blushing like a schoolgirl, but this time it wasn't because of the show. If he didn't know better, he'd have sworn she'd never felt up a man before.

He couldn't help himself. He slid his own hand, which had been perched safely on the back of her chair throughout the show, down her shoulder, letting his fingertips brush the side of her breast. She inhaled sharply, and his arousal grew.

On stage, a marriage-stricken cowboy sang an ode to the good old days of swinging bachelorhood. Judd tried to focus on the show to curb his desire. The cowboy had it all backward. Being a bachelor wasn't the way to live. A man needed a woman to make his life complete.

The photograph of Lucy on the mantel in her apartment came to mind suddenly, out of nowhere. That conservative-looking Lucy was a far cry from what he'd seen of her here at the ranch. The inconsistency nagged at him, and his sensible side wished she were more like that mousy image.

Judd felt a tickling sensation on his earlobe, then a gentle pressure that set his nerves pulsing. It was Lucy. Biting him. Her breath sent tingles down his spine as she nibbled. His fate was in her hands. Whatever she wanted to do, he knew he'd go along with it, no resistance, no questions asked.

Up on stage the show was over, and performers were milling around, practicing dance steps, talking.

"Show's over," Judd whispered, unable to summon his normal voice in the face of such blatant temptation.

"Walk me back to my room?"

"Sure," he said, agreeing to his own downfall.

## 7

LUCY HAD NO IDEA where she'd found the courage to invite Judd back to her room, but here they were. No backing out now. She felt giddy, drunk, apt to say or to do something stupid at any moment. And then she did.

"Hope you're not tired," she joked, holding up the giant box of condoms Claire packed.

Judd was sitting on the bed, tugging on a boot, luckily too engaged in the task to hear her lame attempt at humor. "These things are damn near impossible to get off."

"Need some help?" She dropped the box onto the dresser and went to him.

"If you don't mind." He stuck out his foot, and Lucy straddled it.

"Not the way I usually get romantic with a woman, but—ouch!"

"Sorry." Lucy adjusted her grip on the boot, dug in her heels, and gave it another good tug.

This time the boot came loose and she went sailing backward, landing on her rear end with a thud. Judd hobbled over in his one boot and held out a hand to pull her up.

"How do you get these things off by yourself?"

"They're not usually this bad. Guess my feet are a little swollen."

Lucy eyed the remaining boot and wondered how she'd ever help him remove it and preserve what was left of her dignity. Then she took in the full picture of Judd sitting there in his cowboy bimbo outfit with his one leg stuck out waiting for her, and she realized she didn't have anything to worry about.

"Okay, here goes... Umph!"

She went sailing backward again, Judd's vacated boot in her hand. This time though, as she lay sprawled on the floor, he didn't extend a hand to help her up. Instead, he stood over her for a moment, smiling.

"I'm trying to think how I can best show my appreciation."

She tossed the boot aside, feeling bolder than ever now that she was so close to her goal. "You can't do it from up there."

He knelt. "How about from here?"

"I think you'll have to come closer."

In a blink he was only inches away from her, effectively pinning her to the floor. She could feel the heat radiating from his body, and she could even smell the subtle scent of soap and shampoo from his shower that morning, mingled with his own unique smell that made her dizzy and giddy all at the same time. She wanted to spread her legs to invite him closer, and at the same time the thought of doing that made her tremble with fear.

"I should tell you, as a rule I don't sleep with guests at the ranch."

The breath went out of Lucy's lungs. "I'm the exception?" she whispered.

He reached up and trailed a finger along her jawline. That simple touch made her want to feel his hands everywhere on her, especially all the most sensitive places.

"You're my weakness."

He was flattering her now. She'd never been any man's weakness, not even her ex-fiancé's. She wasn't that good of an actress, either, and no matter how hard she might have tried to seduce Judd, what was happening between them had to be a fluke.

Before Lucy could respond, he pushed her knees apart with his thighs and wedged himself between her legs. His hands slid around her waist under her swimsuit cover-up, and he kissed her. Thoughts swirled in her brain without ever becoming coherent, and she heard herself making little whimpering sounds into his mouth as she opened up to him to return the kiss.

Oh, such heat. Heat coursing through her veins, hanging in the air between them, burning all the places where their bodies met. It was a sweet burning, like a fire after coming in from the cold, and Lucy wanted to warm herself all over with it.

"Judd," she gasped when his mouth found the side of her neck and he began to suck, creating sensations she hadn't known could occur in such an innocuous spot.

If he kept on like this, working her body as if he knew her every weakness, she'd be lost forever, unable to lead a normal life or to think about anything but making love to him. He teased her nipples with his fingertips and used his knee to create a sweet friction between her legs. Lucy could only hold on to his broad shoulders for dear life and pray that she'd remember how this felt when she was old and gray and living as a spinster—living without a man because Judd would surely ruin her for anyone else.

Before she knew what was happening, she felt herself being lifted, and Judd's arms were holding her tightly as he carried her through the patio doors and onto the balcony. When he sat her on the stucco wall, she let out a little whimper. They were on the second floor, and Lucy was already dizzy from their kissing. She refused to let go her grip on him.

"Don't worry, I've got you."

She looked into his eyes and they were half-lidded and smoldering, as if he were on fire for her the way she was for him. The thought seemed too ridiculous to entertain.

She exhaled, shuddering involuntarily at all the sensations that coursed through her.

"What's wrong?"

"I'm afraid of...this."

He placed a soft kiss on her lips. "What are you afraid of?"

He was trailing kisses along her jawline now, and Lucy struggled to produce a coherent sentence. "I—I don't know."

"Are you afraid of me?"

"Yes." Afraid of losing her mind, afraid of becoming addicted to Judd, afraid of never being able to appreciate another man...

He stopped. "Do you mean—"

"No, I shouldn't have said that. I mean I'm afraid of this." She leaned forward and kissed him tentatively. "Anything that feels this good can't be healthy."

"I can assure you it's perfectly healthy." His voice was lower, more gravelly than usual. He brushed a lock of her hair behind her ear and smiled.

"Like broccoli?"

"No." He began to unfasten the little hooks on her cover-up. "More like a banana split. There's that nutritious banana in there, but lots of other good stuff, too."

"I don't eat banana splits." Her own voice sounded tight, and her body throbbed in all the places she wanted him to touch her. "Too unhealthy." She wanted to kick herself for saying something Boring Lucy would say.

He pulled open her swimsuit cover-up, revealing the hot-pink bikini top that barely covered her chest. When Judd let out a ragged breath as he looked at her, she wondered what was wrong with him. Surely her barely-34-B chest couldn't elicit such a response from a man like him.

He trailed his finger across one already-hardened nipple, and Lucy couldn't resist the urge to arch herself toward him.

"You shouldn't worry so much about stuff like that. Sometimes a little whipped cream and strawberry sauce are exactly what you need."

"Maybe you're right," she whispered as he leaned his head down and placed a kiss on the upper half of one breast. Lucy's skin came alive with goose bumps.

A strangled sound erupted from deep within his

## The Harlequin Reader Service® — Here's how it works:

Accepting your 2 free books and gift places you under no obligation to buy anything. You may keep the books and gift and return the shipping statement marked "cancel." If you do not cancel, about a month later we'll send you 4 additional books and bill you just $3.57 each in the U.S., or $4.24 each in Canada, plus 25¢ shipping & handling per book and applicable taxes if any.* That's the complete price and — compared to cover prices of $4.25 each in the U.S. and $4.99 each in Canada — it's quite a bargain! You may cancel at any time, but if you choose to continue, every month we'll send you 4 more books, which you may either purchase at the discount price or return to us and cancel your subscription.

*Terms and prices subject to change without notice. Sales tax applicable in N.Y. Canadian residents will be charged applicable provincial taxes and GST.

If offer card is missing write to: Harlequin Reader Service, 3010 Walden Ave., P.O. Box 1867, Buffalo NY 14240-1867

NO POSTAGE
NECESSARY
IF MAILED
IN THE
UNITED STATES

## BUSINESS REPLY MAIL
FIRST-CLASS MAIL    PERMIT NO. 717-003    BUFFALO, NY

POSTAGE WILL BE PAID BY ADDRESSEE

HARLEQUIN READER SERVICE
3010 WALDEN AVE
PO BOX 1867
BUFFALO NY 14240-9952

# GET FREE BOOKS and a FREE GIFT WHEN YOU PLAY THE...

## Lucky 7

### SLOT MACHINE GAME!

*Just scratch off the silver box with a coin. Then check below to see the gifts you get!*

**YES!** I have scratched off the silver box. Please send me the 2 free Harlequin Temptation® books and gift for which I qualify. I understand I am under no obligation to purchase any books, as explained on the back of this card.

342 HDL DRRP

142 HDL DRR5
(H-T-01/03)

| | |
|---|---|
| FIRST NAME | LAST NAME |

ADDRESS

| | |
|---|---|
| APT.# | CITY |

| | |
|---|---|
| STATE/PROV. | ZIP/POSTAL CODE |

| 7 | 7 | 7 | Worth **TWO FREE BOOKS** plus a **BONUS** Mystery Gift! |
|---|---|---|---|
| 🍒 | 🍒 | 🍒 | Worth **TWO FREE BOOKS!** |
| ♣ | ♣ | ♣ | Worth **ONE FREE BOOK!** |
| 🔔 | 🔔 | 🍒 | **TRY AGAIN!** |

*Visit us online at www.eHarlequin.com*

DETACH AND MAIL CARD TODAY!

throat, and he looked at her again. "You drive me crazy, woman."

Just then she noticed the very obvious bulge in his jean shorts. She'd done that?

"Yeah, that's what you do to me. A lot more often than I'd like to admit. Last night I couldn't sleep because of you, and let me tell you, cold showers are highly overrated."

Cold showers? He'd stayed awake all night taking cold showers because of her? It seemed ridiculous, yet in front of her eyes was the proof.

He wanted her just as badly as she wanted him.

The sparks Lucy felt were real then. The realization was almost enough to jar her out of the moment, to make her forget how badly she wanted to experience Judd completely. Almost.

He pulled her toward him until she hopped off the wall, and then he was undressing her, and she was making a futile attempt to remove his jean shorts, her hands fumbling with the button and zipper. Her mouth found its way to his for another desperate kiss. Before she even had a chance to be embarrassed, she stood naked in front of him, and his gaze took her in from head to toe as he bent to rid himself of his shorts and briefs.

Lucy stared at him. She'd never known before that a man—every single part of him—could be called beautiful, but that was the first word that came to mind when she took in Judd's broad shoulders, his tapering torso, well-tanned and sculpted, his narrow hips, his muscled thighs and his too large, too obvious erection that told her just how he felt at that moment.

He was ready for her, and she felt shaky in the knees at the very thought of him making love to her. He reached for the box of condoms. Finally, she'd met a man she could imagine using that entire box with.

Judd took her hand and led her to the cushioned chaise longue, where he laid down and pulled her on top so that she straddled him. Lucy watched, transfixed, as he removed a condom from the box, tore off the wrapper, then slid it on.

He strained against her, threatening to finish her off before they even got started. But he wanted her on top? A bolt of fear shot through her.

"I've never done it like this..." In fact, she'd never been in any position besides plain old missionary.

Confusion furrowed his brow, but then he seemed to understand. "Don't worry, I'll help."

And he did. He gripped her hips and guided her forward, looking into her eyes the entire time as he led her through the movements. He didn't close his eyes or look away even as he thrust deep inside her, even as he urged her hips into an impossibly slow rocking motion that was the sweetest torture Lucy had ever felt.

The warm evening air and the soft wind only heightened the sensations their bodies made together. Her every nerve was alive and pulsing, her skin felt as if it had been pulled taut and her breasts ached for Judd's mouth. So when he leaned his head forward and took one breast in, sucking and licking and teasing with his tongue, she cried out in a strangled cry loud enough to wake the entire west wing of the hotel.

Loud enough to shock herself, since she'd never once cried out with such abandon during lovemaking.

When he gave his attention to her other breast, Lucy began to feel confident in the once-awkward position. She experimented with different rhythms, faster, slower—and she was shocked when Judd fell back onto the longue, gasping in apparent ecstasy at her movements.

She watched the pleasure that played across his face in awe. *She* was doing that to him. *She* had the power to turn a man like Judd into a gasping, moaning prisoner of her body. It was the most enlightening revelation she'd ever had, and if her own body wasn't responding with such force to their lovemaking, she might have had time to revel in it.

But Judd grasped her hips, and as he began to thrust more quickly himself, Lucy matched his movements. He filled her, stretched her, made her body accommodate his in the sweetest way possible. And as her muscles tightened around him in a series of shattering contractions, she looked into his eyes and cried out again, this time with a sureness she barely recognized as her own.

Judd released into her, his every muscle tensed, and then after a long sweet moment, completely relaxed. He was glazed with a film of perspiration that glistened in the half-light, and Lucy tasted it on his neck as she rested on top of him and nestled her face next to his own.

So this was what it felt like to have great sex. This was what all those rock and roll songs were written about. Lucy smiled. This was far, far better than she'd imagined it could be.

But, Lucy realized, she had no idea what sorts of things to say to a man with whom she'd just shared a meaningless sexual encounter. Unfortunately—or fortunately, she couldn't decide—she didn't get a chance to try out any of her chosen topics. Judd's employee cell phone rang only minutes after they'd exhausted themselves, with an urgent call from his brother. He told his brother he was busy and couldn't be disturbed again, but Lucy encouraged him to go. After all, he'd already endangered his job because of her. She'd hate to see him get fired.

So he went. Now she was alone, left to wonder why their meaningless sex didn't feel meaningless at all. No, she was quite sure something profound had just happened to her, but she was afraid to kid herself into thinking the blissful look on Judd's face before he'd left meant that he felt the same thing.

Lucy turned on the hot tub and climbed in once it started to fill up. She was amazed at how tired she felt. She slid down, letting the steaming, bubbly water envelope her body. This was just what she needed, time to reflect, time to get used to the idea that Boring Lucy was gone forever. Wild-and-Crazy Lucy was here to stay, and she couldn't get her mind off of Judd.

One little sexual fantasy couldn't hurt...

They were in the desert, with no one around for miles. Up on a high cliff, overlooking the harsh landscape and a brilliant sunset. Judd's hands were massaging her, slipping under items of clothing and then slowly removing them. He was planting little butter-fly kisses all over her belly—

*Bang, bang, bang.*

"Lucy, let me in!"

She squeezed her eyes shut tight. Maybe the interruption would go away. Now, where had she left off?

"Lucy? It's Claire. We need to talk right now!"

She supposed she wouldn't be much of a friend if she let Claire stand out in the hallway for another hour or so. With a weary sigh, she climbed out of the tub, grabbing a giant bath towel to wrap around herself on her way to the door.

"You've got lousy timing," she said as Claire breezed in and stopped to give her a suspicious look.

"I didn't interrupt anything juicy, did I?"

"Not exactly."

She frowned. "It figures."

Lucy tightened the towel and sat on the nearest chair, deciding she would wait a while to reveal her encounter with Judd. She needed time to get used to the idea herself. "So what's all the commotion about?"

"That guy you told me about, Judd Walker? I thought it sounded strange that they didn't send Buck like I asked, so I did some checking around after we got off the phone."

Claire clicked her long red fingernails together as she talked, a nervous habit she'd picked up when she quit smoking.

"I don't understand. What kind of checking around?"

"I just wanted to see what his deal was. Turns out

he's listed in the Phoenix white pages—Judd Walker, Private Investigator."

Lucy's head spun. "But..."

"Something fishy's going on here, Lucy!"

"I don't understand. Why would Judd be listed as a private investigator?"

"Because he *is* one."

"But he's an employee here at the ranch. How could he do both jobs? Or is he investigating something here?"

"That's what I'm trying to figure out. I mean, he couldn't be investigating you—your life's too boring to warrant it."

"Gee, thanks."

"I think you should stay away from him, just to be careful. Who knows what he's doing."

"It must be a different Judd Walker."

"Sure, Luc. The name Judd is real common, right up there with Mike and John."

Judd, a private investigator? There had to be a mistake. "You're being paranoid." For an intelligent woman, Claire had a strong paranoia streak.

"No, I'm not. There's got to be something funny going on here. I've been thinking about it all the way from Phoenix, and I've got a few ideas—"

"This is all some kind of misunderstanding. The Judd Walker I know is a gorgeous male bimbo who can barely hold down a job."

Claire stopped clicking her nails together and looked at Lucy as if she were seeing her for the first time. "Where did that rosy glow come from? And that

redness around your mouth! I did interrupt something interesting!''

''I was just taking a bath.''

''Are you hiding a man in there?'' Claire peered into
the bathroom, then turned back to Lucy with her eyes
narrowed.

''There's no one in there!''

Claire flashed a triumphant smile. ''You've got the
glow! You just had sex.''

Lucy felt heat creeping up her neck and then her
face. ''Is it that obvious?''

In an instant her smile faded. ''Wait a minute,
though—it wasn't with that detective guy, was it?''

''He's not a detective, and yes, it was with him.'' In
spite of her words, a little sliver of doubt had worked
its way in.

Claire's eyes widened, and she began to rattle on
about what a private investigator might be doing
hanging around Lucy at the resort.

Lucy tuned her out as she dug an outfit out of the
closet and got dressed. What if Judd had been deceiving her these past few days? What if he wasn't what he
seemed at all? What if she was the object of some investigation he was conducting? What if the incredible
sex they'd just had was all a part of his cover?

No. First, Claire was right that her life was far too
boring to warrant investigation, and second, Judd
seemed genuine, not like someone putting on an act.

''Lucy, are you listening to me? Whatever you do,
don't let him know that you know he's a detective.''

Lucy sighed. It would do no good to argue with
Claire when she was in this state of mind. ''Fine.''

But she had no choice. She had to see the look on his face when she mentioned Claire's discovery. She had to be certain he was just the male bimbo he said he was, and nothing more.

"By the way, I'm bunking in your room."

"You are?"

"The ranch was booked through the weekend when I called, because of the end-of-summer celebration, so I figured you wouldn't mind."

"Not at all."

Claire had paid for the trip, after all, so she couldn't very well complain about a little loss of privacy, and now that she was staying in a suite, there was more than enough room for the two of them.

"Besides, I can better supervise your party-girl efforts from here—make sure you're not hanging out in your room all night reading or anything."

"You'd be proud, Claire. I've had more fun this weekend than I have in a long, long time."

Claire smiled as she examined herself in the nearby dresser mirror. "Good girl!"

"Thanks for my birthday present," Lucy said as Claire hugged her. "I never would have done this without your, um, little nudge."

"That's what friends are for."

"I'll be back in a little while," Lucy said as she headed for the door, hoping to avoid questioning.

"If I'm not here when you get back, I'll be out looking for Buck. I've got to meet the man one of my clients called God's gift to leather pants."

JUDD SWUNG OPEN THE DOOR to his brother's office, half hoping Mason was standing behind it so he could give him a good smack in the head. Instead, Mason was seated at his desk, staring at the computer screen.

"There's been an interesting development, bro."

"It better be earth-shattering—not just interesting." He hadn't wanted to leave. He'd wanted to stay and make love to Lucy again and again, to fall asleep in her arms, and to wake up there, too. That was why he'd been willing to leave.

The feelings were too intense. In Lucy's company he'd forgotten all about the promises he'd made to himself. For a short time he hadn't cared that she might only be interested in his body.

And for her, it really was just sex. She'd proven her lack of interest in anything more by insisting he go on his way as soon as Mason called. No pillow talk for her.

His ego had suffered more than a little bruising to have a woman he'd just thoroughly made love to casually dismiss him from her room. Had their lovemaking been less intense for her than it was for him? He'd always thought he could gauge a woman's pleasure, but Lucy had him doubting that ability—among others.

Yet he had gotten to know her a little better in those brief moments. She was raw sex and innocence rolled into one irresistible package. It wasn't an act. It was her secret weapon, against which he was defenseless.

"I think you'll find it worthy of the trip down here." Mason continued to glare at the computer screen.

"I just had an interesting development of my own." Judd paused for effect. "Lucy's not involved."

His brother finally looked at him squarely. "You got any hard proof of that?"

No, but he wasn't ready to share his theory about the real perpetrator with Mason. Not until he had a better handle on it.

"I've searched her entire room without finding any hint of criminal wrongdoing, and I've been with her almost constantly since she arrived. She's not scheming for the downfall of your business. I've got all the proof I need."

Saying it out loud made it feel all the more true, and Judd felt a sense of relief that Lucy wasn't involved in anything clandestine.

"Then how do you explain the fact that the general manager of Sunny Horizons Travel just tried to check into a room here for the rest of the week?"

"Claire Elliot? The one that handcuffed me to Lucy's bed?"

"That would be her. We're booked solid, so she inquired about Lucy's room number."

Judd quelled the rising doubt about Lucy's innocence. "What's she doing here?"

"It's your job to find out, so get to it. If they're planning something big for the end-of-summer celebration, you've got to make sure it doesn't happen."

Judd was beginning to wonder exactly how difficult narrowing down his brother's list of possible enemies would be. Mason could be a real pain in the butt. "Is that all you called me down here for?"

"Isn't that enough?"

Judd turned on his heel and walked out before he

succumbed to the urge to strangle his brother. The best way to find out more about Claire's arrival would be through Lucy. It didn't hurt that she was the person he most wanted to see anyway.

# 8

LUCY ROUNDED THE CORNER of the hallway and ran into a wall of flesh. Large hands grasped her shoulders, steadying her when she bounced off. She looked up to see Judd's face inches away.

"Whoa, there, just the girl I'm looking for."

"I'm looking for you!"

He smiled. "That's good news. We need to talk. How about back in your room?"

Okay, no problem. She could be alone with him for a few minutes without stripping him naked and demanding a repeat performance of their lovemaking. Then she remembered Claire, who may or may not have been out searching for Buck.

"It's not private. I've got a roommate now."

"A roommate?"

"You've met her. Claire, the one who let you in my apartment?"

His eyebrows perked. "She's here?"

Lucy nodded. "Yep, she decided to join me for the rest of the week."

"Let's go for a walk then," he said.

They left the building and began following a rock path that wound its way across the resort, surrounded by gardens.

"Claire told me something about you," Lucy said,

deciding to go for the straightforward approach. "I told her she's crazy, but she says you're a private investigator."

Out of the corner of her eye, she saw the muscle in his jaw working. "Where'd she hear that?"

He wasn't laughing in shock or denying it as she'd expected. Lucy tried to ignore the hurt she felt. "Is it true?"

Silence. "I guess it's okay to tell you, but you have to promise to keep it to yourself." He paused. "And, you have to somehow convince Claire that I'm really just an employee here at the ranch."

"Are you saying she's right?"

"It's true, I'm a private investigator."

Lucy's feet stopped moving. Her stomach tightened into a little ball. All the bliss of a few hours ago disappeared, and the hurt turned into anger.

"I need to know how she found out."

"You lied to me? You pretended to be someone you weren't and you slept with me." Her voice was rising, becoming shaky and squeaky at the same time. She hated the way she sounded when she was upset.

"Not exactly. I just lied about my profession, not who I am, and I had good reason to do it."

"Are you investigating me?"

"I was, but I'm not now."

"Oh, so what happened this afternoon marked the conclusion of your investigation?"

"Not at all."

Glaring at him, she felt tears form in her eyes. She wouldn't cry; absolutely would not cry. Blinking, she demanded, "Why?"

"Why don't you calm down. I can't tell you why right now."

"You...you jerk!"

She spun around and ran, not sure where she was headed.

"Lucy! Damn it, come back here." A pause. "Okay, don't. I'll talk to you when you've calmed down."

By the time she made it to her room, Claire was relaxing on her bed drinking wine from the suite's wet bar.

"This place is great. How'd you end up in a suite?"

"I don't want to talk about it. I'm leaving, so you can have this room if you want it."

She went to the closet, pulled out her suitcase, and started yanking clothes off of hangers.

"You're not leaving, you just got started having fun!"

"I've had enough fun for one birthday. This place isn't for me."

Claire started pulling things back out of the bag, and Lucy threw up her hands. "I'll just leave all this stuff here. It'll look better on you anyway."

Grabbing her purse from the dresser, she headed for the door.

"Wait, Lucy. What happened? What's wrong?"

She remembered Claire's admonition not to let Judd know she knew about his profession, so she said, "I'm not cut out for casual sex. It's time for me to go."

"But—"

Lucy gave her friend a squeeze. "I'm going, no arguments. But I don't have any transportation. Can I take your car and pick you up at the end of the week?"

Claire frowned at her. It was a testament to the depth of their friendship that she finally nodded and dug the keys out of her own purse. She loved her car as if it were her child. "Be good to Daisy, and feed her only premium gas."

Lucy found her way to the resort's main entrance, and was about to ask someone which lot was for guest parking when she spotted a familiar form behind the registration counter. Judd. He was talking to the desk clerk, and he had just spotted her. She turned and headed for the door.

"Lucy, wait up!"

Outside, she saw the sign for guest parking and followed it. Behind her the sound of feet pounding on the sidewalk came closer and closer.

"We've got to talk."

"No, we don't."

A bus had just pulled up and a load of gray-haired tourists was pouring out. Lucy wound her way through the crowd, trying to lose Judd, but she was stopped by a gaggle of grandfatherly men in skintight jeans, Western shirts, Stetsons and cowboy boots.

"Hey, sweetcakes, take our picture, okay?" one of the men asked, shoving the camera into her hand.

"No, no! She should be in the picture," his friend insisted, motioning for Lucy to join the posing group. "Get that guy to take it."

Judd frowned as the camera was thrust into his hands, but he obliged the group. "Okay, I'll count to three, then everyone smile and say 'hot sex.'"

"One, two, three..."

"Hot sex!" the group repeated with a little more enthusiasm than Lucy cared to consider.

She involuntarily grimaced just as the camera flashed. Someone gave her a pat on the rear end, and she spun around to see a smiling man old enough to be her grandfather. "Hot sex," he repeated, nodding and wiggling his eyebrows.

"No thanks."

She veered off toward the parking lot, but Judd caught up with her.

"You're leaving?"

"Try not to take it personally."

"I'm sorry, Lucy. Really, really sorry. I had no choice but to hide my profession from you."

Lucy spotted Claire's bright red convertible three aisles over and turned that way. "I'm just not cut out for this place. I don't fit in here. It's better if I leave."

"You're leaving because you're mad at me. I can't let you do that."

"You don't have a choice."

"Please, Lucy. Stay and have a good time."

She unlocked the car door, but Judd slipped between her and the convertible and leaned against it, blocking her entry.

"There's another door on the other side, you know."

"I can move faster than you."

"Get out of my way!"

"Just listen to me. I had to keep my investigation a secret to help my brother. I never meant to deceive you."

She looked him in the eye and saw nothing there

but earnestness. Maybe she was a fool, but he seemed to mean what he said. He really looked sorry, and the pained expression he wore tugged at her heart. Judd was even more impossible to resist when he was pleading for forgiveness.

"You're just helping your brother? You swear?"

"I swear."

An investigation. It sounded so intriguing, so exciting, so much more interesting than any entertainment the Fantasy Ranch had to offer. She wanted to know all the juicy details.

"Tell me about your investigation, and I'll forgive you."

Judd chewed on his lip, raked his fingers through his hair. "Um, I really can't do that."

"Why not?" The wheels in her head were spinning faster than ever now. Maybe he *was* investigating her. Maybe that's why he didn't want her to leave!

"I need to maintain my cover to help Mason."

"I can be trusted with a secret."

"I believe you." He smiled and reached for her hand. "But I can't tell you any details right now. Maybe later."

"If you're a detective, that means you're not a male bimbo at all!"

"Bimbo?"

"You know what I mean. I just assumed you were an empty-headed pretty-boy," Lucy admitted, realizing suddenly that perhaps sex with Judd was more complicated than she'd expected it to be.

"Thanks."

"You didn't do anything to discourage that notion. How long have you been a detective, anyway?"

Judd sighed. "I guess I can answer that one. I opened my private investigation business two years ago after I was forced to quit the police force."

"You were a police officer!"

"For ten years. And then I stupidly had a one-night stand with my boss's girlfriend. I didn't know she was his girl until it was too late."

"He found out?"

"I told him. They were on a 'break,' but needless to say, he wasn't happy, and I found myself permanently working traffic patrol. Six months of that and I did exactly what he wanted me to—I quit."

"Wow."

"Any more questions?"

"What were you really doing in my room on my birthday?"

"Giving you your birthday surprise."

"I think I caught you doing some investigating."

She pulled her hand away and crossed her arms over her chest.

"There's no use trying to pry anything else out of me." And then a half smile touched his lips. "Well, you could try. You're welcome to try. Torture, seduction, whatever you think is necessary."

"You were investigating me, weren't you? I caught you in the act on my birthday, and the kiss was just your means of distracting me from the truth."

"I kissed you because I wanted to."

She wanted desperately to believe him, but she also wanted the truth.

"If you don't tell me what's going on, I'm going to announce to the whole resort that you're a detective here conducting some clandestine operation."

"Why would you go and do something like that?"

"Because you riffled through my underwear drawer. Because you slept with me under false pretenses. Because you lied to me."

There, she'd stated her case. He'd be crazy to refuse her. Lucy needed something fun to do for the rest of the week, and he needed someone like her to help with whatever it was he was doing.

"Lucy, there's a more important reason Claire might have been motivated to check me out. She must know that I'm on to her. I've ruled you out as a suspect, but Claire is likely involved."

Suspects? Motivation? This was getting stranger by the minute. "Involved in what?"

"A plot to ruin Fantasy Ranch's business."

Lucy's head spun. This wasn't making sense at all. "What on earth are you talking about?"

Judd gave her a speculative look. "How do I know I can trust you?"

She shrugged. "I'm a trustworthy kind of girl."

"If you turn out not to be trustworthy, I'll make sure every guy vacationing here knows about that gigantic box of condoms in your room. You'll have more potential one-night stands than you'd know what to do with."

"That's a dirty trick."

Once Judd had explained to her the connection between Sunny Horizons Travel and the Fantasy

Ranch's biggest competitor, the Oasis Spa and Resort, she understood how they'd come to be investigated.

"Claire's not involved."

"How can you be so sure? She did go to the trouble to look up my credentials."

"I know her. You're looking in the wrong place."

"Who could it be then?"

"You're the sleuth. Haven't you checked the records of who from the agency has stayed here since the sabotage began?"

"Of course I have, but I want to know who you'd suspect."

Lucy bit her lip. Could one or more of her co-workers really be guilty of trying to ruin the ranch? "I haven't been working there very long, so I don't know the other travel agents well."

"Take a wild guess."

"Hmm…Frank Wiley has shifty eyes."

Judd made a mental note to check him out further, but he laughed. "In serious investigations, I have to go on more than just shifty eyes."

"Well, give me a minute to think… I've heard Carol Banks talk about visiting here fairly often. Maybe she could be involved."

"She could be a possibility. Have you heard any of your co-workers discouraging their customers from coming here?"

"Maybe—I don't know. It's not something I'd ever note as unusual if I did hear it."

"Anyone you know of that's personally acquainted with the CEO of Sunset Enterprises, Natasha Kendrick?"

Lucy had a vague memory of someone talking about what a babe Natasha Kendrick was. "Darren Ullrich! He met her at a Sunset Enterprises Christmas party, I think. Came to work talking about how hot she was."

"Tell me more about this Darren guy."

"He's young, in his late twenties. Kind of a slacker—I think Claire only keeps him around the agency as eye candy, because he's quite attractive."

Judd seemed to be pondering this new information. After a few moments of silence he asked, "Attractive enough to garner the attention of someone like Natasha?"

"Sure, I guess."

He smiled. "I think we may have something there."

We? Did that mean he was going to let her help him? She suppressed a little smile. She really hadn't given him a whole lot of choice in the matter.

"Wait a minute, though. Isn't the sabotage still going on?"

Judd nodded.

"And I'm the only one from the agency staying here right now besides Claire."

"Yep."

"There's got to be someone else. An insider."

"Meaning?"

"An employee at the ranch. Maybe someone who's disgruntled, wants to get even."

"That's what I've been thinking. It would explain how whoever's responsible has access to so many areas without being spotted by other employees."

"See, I'm going to be a big help to you."

"I don't really need any help."

"You thought I was a suspect, didn't you? Seems to me you need a lot of help."

Judd stood, reached out and pulled her to him, his sudden nearness creating a butterfly frenzy in her belly. "You're a pretty shady character, Lucinda Connors."

"Don't call me Lucinda."

He traced her jawline with one finger. "But it fits."

"It's too old-fashioned," she whispered, suddenly conscious of her breasts pressing against his chest, of the pressure of his pelvis against her abdomen. She wanted to tear his clothes off.

"It's unique, like you. Beautiful and unique."

Had he just called her beautiful? She didn't have time to think about it because he lowered his lips to hers then, rendering her senseless.

LUCY CONNORS, PRIVATE EYE, had a nice ring to it. Lucy smiled as she made her way down the hall, heading to Judd's room. It had been two days since she'd seen him, and for such a casual, meaningless sexual relationship, she sure did miss being around him. It had to be her libido responding to long-term deprivation.

Sunday night he'd had to do work that he claimed Lucy couldn't help with, leaving her to tag along with Claire on her evening out flirting with half the men at the ranch. She'd kept a lookout for Judd everywhere they went, hoping to run into him while he was working, but no luck. Instead she'd spent the evening warding off sexual advances from Claire's rejects and puzzling over the feeling that Judd had given her the brush-off.

Then Monday, Lucy had talked Claire into going on an all-day excursion to some nearby ancient Native American ruins. Lucy had always wanted to view them, and in spite of Claire's complaints that they were losing out on valuable man-hunting time, they'd both found the ruins fascinating.

By the time they'd gotten back to the ranch and eaten dinner, they had both fallen into bed exhausted from the desert heat. Lucy had hoped to see a message from Judd waiting for her, but no luck. He was busy, though, she understood, and his time was running out to find the culprit behind the sabotage.

But still, she couldn't help wondering if he'd missed her as much as she'd missed him.

She stopped at Judd's door and knocked. She'd decided to drop in and surprise him, but now she was wondering if he'd appreciate an unannounced visitor.

Judd opened the door and blinked at her. "Oh, hi," he said, sounding distracted.

He had a day's growth of beard, and his hair was uncombed, giving him the look of a man who'd just rolled out of bed. Lucy glanced at her watch. It was past eleven in the morning.

"I'm sorry, did I wake you?"

"No, I've just been going over my case files all morning and haven't stopped to shave or shower yet."

He stepped aside and motioned for her to come in.

Lucy slipped past him, her nipples perking up at his nearness. She admired the muscles of his back rippling under his T-shirt as he cleared off a chair for her, and then she sat at the table, opposite his laptop computer.

Judd sat at the computer and glared at the screen for a moment before closing it. "Where did you disappear to yesterday?"

"Wouldn't you like to know, detective," she said in her best vixen voice, feeling silly before the words had even finished rolling off her tongue.

Something about Judd's mood felt off.

"I thought you were going to help me. I can't watch Claire if you hide her from me."

"We decided at the last minute to take one of the bus excursions to the Salado ruins. And she can't be involved in the sabotage if she's out hiking around in the middle of the desert."

He looked at her as if she'd just professed a love for Barry Manilow's music. "Are you trying to thwart my investigation?"

"No, I want to help. Just tell me what I can do."

"For starters, keep your friend from running off anywhere."

"Got it." But she didn't get it. Why was he in such a foul mood? "What's wrong?"

Judd leaned back in his chair and ran his fingers through his scruffy hair. "It's just this investigation frustrating me."

"No breakthroughs yet?"

He shook his head. "I feel like I'm backpedaling."

Lucy glanced around at the empty carry-out containers scattered around the room, at least three meals' worth. "It looks like it's time for you to get out of this room. Let's go have lunch and then get to work solving your case."

She slapped her hands on her thighs to punctuate the statement and then stood. "Come on, get cleaned up so we can go."

"I wish I could have lunch with you, but I've got some more work to do here."

"Then we'll order in."

Judd shook his head and opened his laptop again. "I need to concentrate. I'm sorry."

Lucy kept her expression neutral, but her heart pounded double-time in her chest. He was brushing her off. This sort of thing wasn't supposed to happen to Wild-and-Crazy Lucy, but she had a feeling Wild-and-Crazy Lucy wasn't supposed to feel rejected if it did. No, *she'd* turn the situation to her advantage...somehow. But unfortunately Boring Lucy had taken over again, hurt feelings and all.

She shrugged and plastered a smile on her face. "I'd better get going then."

Judd stopped glaring at the computer screen and looked up at Lucy as if he had just noticed her standing there. "I really am sorry. Maybe I'll see you later."

With what she hoped was an air of mystery, she said, "Maybe you will."

Lucy let herself out of the room, waving a casual goodbye as she went, and closed the door behind her. She stood alone in the hallway, trying not to feel sorry for herself. What had just happened in there?

She replayed in her mind the last time she'd seen Judd, tried to remember if she'd said or done anything to offend him. Maybe this was just how he treated women with whom he'd had meaningless sex. Maybe now that he'd had a few days away from her, the magic had worn off and he was no longer interested.

Lucy wandered outside into the bright noonday sun and slipped on her sunglasses. She was not going to pout, and she was not going to feel sorry for herself. Whatever Judd's problem was, he could keep it to himself. He obviously didn't understand how much help she could be in his investigation.

Perhaps it really was just the unsolved mystery of the sabotage that had Judd in a cranky mood. And if that was the case, helping him solve it, whether he wanted her help or not, would cheer him up. Besides, she didn't have anything more interesting to do here at the ranch than play private investigator.

Lucy made a beeline for the pool, where Claire had said she would be spending the afternoon. Her first task would be to watch Claire and to prove her friend had nothing to do with the sabotage.

# 9

NOW THAT HE had an uninvited assistant, Judd's life was a lot more complicated. He had to figure out what he could reveal to Lucy and what he couldn't. He had eliminated her as a suspect, but he had no idea how much she could be trusted with information, especially with her best friend being a suspect.

And he didn't know how to keep a clear head with Lucy around. The more time he spent with her, the more he realized he'd grown too fond of her company, too comfortable with her, too preoccupied with thoughts of her all day—and all night.

They'd spent all day Wednesday together, following up on leads and finding nothing but dead ends. Lucy had turned out to be a real help, aside from the little matter of his being unable to think straight with her around.

She'd managed to connect several facts Judd had missed on his own, and her fresh perspective on the case had given Judd a renewed sense of hope that he could solve it in time. She was a fast learner, and an efficient assistant, but she was too sexy for her own good.

It had taken all Judd's willpower not to take her to bed and forget all about the case. The one fact that had kept him in line was that he had only a few days left to

find the saboteurs before the end-of-summer celebration.

Now he needed to focus his efforts exclusively on
who the inside saboteur was, but at the same time he
had to keep an eye on Claire, who'd been spending
quite a bit of time with Buck Samson. He'd been out
late every night trying to monitor Claire's activities, all
the while also trying to avoid the temptation of Lucy.

He felt awful for having brushed her off several
times in the past few days. It was a pitiful attempt on
his part to regain some sense of his former resolve.
Ever since the last time they'd kissed, Judd had felt
some vital part of himself changing, being shaped by
his desire for Lucy. It scared the hell out of him.

He vacillated between aching for her presence and
wishing he'd never met her. So far she'd been un-
daunted by his rudeness, instead insisting on playing
his detective sidekick. Even when he'd behaved like a
total jerk the morning she showed up at his room,
Lucy had still been a good sport. After she'd left, Judd
decided he'd just have to live with the temptation,
since the alternative meant treating Lucy badly.

Ranch guests milled around near Judd as he sat in
the lobby of the Hacienda building trying to blend in.
He'd strategically placed himself beside a large palm
plant that partially blocked anyone's view of him as
he half pretended to read the paper. He was waiting
for Claire to come out of her room and make a move.

"Judd? Judd, is that you?"

Lucy again. She'd found him.

"Shh! Keep your voice down."

"Why are you ducking behind this plant?" She sat next to him on the couch.

"Be quiet."

"Right, sorry. Who are you waiting for?"

"Who do you think?"

"You're wasting your time if you're trying to catch Claire. She's not involved."

"I have to prove that before I can be so sure."

Across the lobby from them, two women wearing thong bikinis were rubbing suntan lotion on two men who were also wearing thong bikinis.

"I've seen enough thongs here to last me the rest of my life," Lucy said, mirroring Judd's thoughts.

And that was when Claire appeared in his peripheral vision, heading toward the main entrance.

He turned to Lucy. "You can't help me with this. You're too easy for her to spot."

"Then I'll go find out what she's doing." She started after Claire and Judd grabbed her wrist.

"No, if you're around her, she's not going to risk doing anything."

"She won't be doing anything because she's innocent."

Just then he realized how Lucy could be of help to him with Claire. Claire wouldn't do anything shady with her around. She could make sure Claire stayed out of trouble while Judd tried to find the other saboteur.

"Go ahead. I'll catch up with you later."

She gave him a suspicious look for suddenly acquiescing, but Claire was already out the door and headed across the front lawn, so she had no time to argue. With a little wave back to him she took off after her friend, leaving Judd to contemplate how fabulous she looked from behind, and how far he was from closing this joke of a case.

He spent the rest of the day on paperwork, first reviewing employee records, trying to find likely candidates for disgruntlement. He'd come up with a good lead after seeing the long list of altercations with management in Buck Samson's file, but this was the kind of tedious, boring attention to detail that most of his work involved. Yet the title "private investigator" always managed to sound exciting and dangerous to the uninitiated.

He read and reread the list of past Sunny Horizons Travel Agency employees who'd stayed at the ranch, and he found several names to investigate further.

By the time his eyes ached and his stomach demanded nourishment, Lucy had managed to find him yet again. This time, though, her presence was more welcome than ever since she came bearing take-out food.

"Hope you don't mind my ordering dinner for you. Baby back ribs, coleslaw, home fries, beer."

He took the bags from her and smiled. "Mind? I could kiss you. In fact, I will kiss you." He leaned forward, resisting the urge to devour her instead of dinner, and planted a light kiss on her lips. His body responded a little too eagerly.

With her head still tilted back and her eyes closed, she stood for a moment too long after he pulled away, looking as if she'd just tasted something heavenly. For such a little vixen, she sure managed to project a convincing aura of innocence.

"Sorry, we'll have to eat fast. Mason has me scheduled to work tonight. My shift starts in a half hour."

"Bummer. That's okay, though. Claire's been begging me to go to some ridiculous wet boxers competition with her tonight. Have you heard of this thing?"

"Unfortunately, yeah, I know all about it. There's a wet lingerie competition, too. Maybe you could enter." He gave her a speculative look and she laughed.

"Right, me in a lingerie competition? That's a good one."

"Modesty sounds ridiculous on a woman like you."

She averted her eyes and if he wasn't mistaken, she blushed, too.

Lucy took their dinner outside on the balcony table, and with the sun setting behind the desert mountains in the west, it made a perfect dinner spot.

They sat across from one another and Judd dug into his ribs. One of the ranch's specialty dishes, they were some of the best he'd ever had. Also the messiest.

"I was with Claire all afternoon, and she never once did anything suspicious. I told you she's not involved."

"What makes you think she would do anything in your presence?"

"Because we're best friends. She trusts me." She took a drink of beer and then grimaced. "Ugh, how do you drink this stuff?"

"It's an acquired taste, and the fact that she's your best friend is exactly why she wouldn't want to involve you in anything illegal. She's trying to protect you."

"I don't buy that. Claire may be a little wild—okay, a lot wild—but she's got a good heart. She wouldn't involve herself in a plot to ruin Mason's business."

"Okay, bear with me 'cause I'm working on a theory here... Why is she hanging around Buck so much? And why did she choose Buck specifically to pick you up if she didn't have some connection to him already?"

"What does Buck have to do with all of this?"

"I'll explain in a minute. First tell me about Claire and Buck."

"She just had a few drinks with him, wanted to see what all the fuss was about. She heard about him from someone at the travel agency, I think."

Judd nodded. A note in the resort's reservation system said Claire had mentioned when she called to book Buck that she'd heard of him through the grapevine, so Lucy's version matched up. Still, he would need some kind of proof before he could be sure Claire wasn't involved in the sabotage.

"So they're not sleeping together?"

"No, he's just eye candy. For all her wild talk, Claire likes a man with some substance."

"I think Buck's the inside guy. I just need some hard evidence."

"I don't think you'll learn anything through Claire."

"We'll just have to agree to disagree on this issue until I know more."

Lucy opened her mouth to protest again, but he

reached across the table and ran his finger over her chin.

"You've got a little barbecue sauce there." He let his hand linger, and she caught it in hers and brought his finger to her mouth, then licked off the sauce.

It was an incredibly arousing gesture, but she looked unsure of herself as she did it. Judd instantly regretted having touched her, because now he wanted to do so much more.

*Down boy, down!* If he ever wanted to solve this case and get the hell away from the Fantasy Ranch, he was going to have to learn to live with the temptation of Lucy for a little while. Somehow.

They finished their dinner together without arguing any further about Claire. While Judd cleaned up, Lucy called Claire's room to let her know that she would be going out with her for the night, and he got a sick feeling in his belly.

Why did the thought of her being at that wet boxers fiasco sound like such a bad idea? He couldn't say, but something told him he'd later regret it.

He made it to the Idle Spurs Lounge five minutes late, just late enough for the lounge manager to notice his absence.

"Where've you been, Mr. Walker? Being the owner's brother doesn't give you special permission to work whatever hours you please, does it?"

Judd gritted his teeth. According to the cover story Mason had given him, he was Mason's irresponsible younger brother who couldn't get a job that wasn't handed to him by his brother. This was Mason's idea of a good joke, and it forced Judd to put up with whatever the managers at the resort decided to do with him.

"No, sir. Sorry I'm late, sir."

Chazz Martinelli, the lounge manager, was not accustomed to being called sir, especially not by Judd. He looked suspicious of the overly polite title, but said nothing about it.

"I'd better warn you now, we sometimes come up short on men for the wet boxers competition, so you may be asked to participate. Remember, this kind of thing is part of the job."

Yeah, Mason had warned him, but he never thought it would come to this. Especially not with Lucy watching.

"For now, though, you'll be waiting tables."

Great. He couldn't think which would be worse, being stuck toting drinks back and forth to horny drunks or being stuck on stage airing his privates to the world. Then he thought of Lucy in the audience again... His privates, definitely his privates.

"CLAIRE, I am not going to put on some little scrap of lingerie and parade around in front of half this resort!"

"Fine, be a stick in the mud if you want."

"I will."

Claire stepped out of the bathroom wearing a purple satin-and-lace bustier with matching panties and garter belt. She did a little twirl. "So what do you think? This or the red teddy?"

"You look great in either one, but at least the teddy leaves something to the imagination."

"Then I'll wear this one."

Lucy sighed. "Sometimes I wish I had your complete lack of modesty, but mostly I'm glad I have more sense than you."

"No you're not. Admit it, you want to enter the contest, too."

"I do not!"

"Okay, fine. I won't push. Besides, if you enter with that little vegetable-eating figure of yours, I won't have a chance of winning."

Lucy laughed. "What's the grand prize?"

"Actually, it's not that kind of contest. It's more of a dating game, without all the dumb questions." Claire disappeared into the bathroom to change back into her street clothes, and Lucy checked her hair in the mirror. Still as untamable as ever.

"I don't understand."

Through the closed door Claire explained. "All the contestants line up in their lingerie, then each one is hosed down and gets her turn to sashay across the stage and back. At the end there's an auction to benefit desert wildlife preservation."

"An auction of what?"

"Of the contestants, silly!"

"You mean..."

"The guys in the audience bid on chances to go out on a date with each contestant, highest bidder wins a date. Then the contestant that commands the highest bid of the competition wins an all-expenses-paid date with her highest bidder."

"That sounds humiliating."

"No, it sounds like fun!" Claire reappeared wearing

a little black dress and strappy high heels that a lesser woman would break her neck in. "I just need to make one call before we leave."

Lucy sat on the edge of the bed and listened as her friend dialed a phone number and asked for the resort manager. What was Claire up to now?

"Yes, can you tell me where one of your employees is working tonight? His name is Judd Walker." A pause. "Yes, mmm-hmm. Thank you."

"What's going on, Claire?"

"He's watching us—I just know it—so we have to keep an eye on him." She hung up the phone.

"He's not watching us!" Lucy imagined her nose growing as she spoke.

"I think he is, and I have a feeling he's using you to get to me." Claire drummed her fingers on the desktop. "I knew I never should have gotten involved with that weird security freak guy. Now he's got a P.I. following me because he's afraid I'm stalking him."

She shook her head at Claire's crazy logic. "What did you do to make him think that?"

"Nothing."

"*Claire?*"

"Okay, maybe I left a few threatening messages on his answering machine, but that was only because he scratched Daisy."

Lucy hated to think what might happen to anyone who did greater damage than a scratch to Claire's much-adored red convertible.

"Is that all you did?"

"Well, maybe I slashed all his tires, too, but that's it, I swear!"

"You really think he'd hire a detective to track your every move?"

"Yes, and lucky for us, Judd's working the lounge tonight, so we'll be in the perfect position to watch him watching us."

Lucy sighed and followed her friend out the door. How could she continue with her plan to seduce Judd when Claire was convinced he was out to get them?

"GUYS AND GALS, our next contestant on stage is Claire. A 36-C who loves skinny-dipping and men with big muscles, Claire's ready to party!"

For once, Lucy was thankful she didn't have Claire's sense of adventure. Up on stage, her friend shimmied around in nothing but her purple lingerie, for the whole world—or at least the whole crowded bar—to see.

A brawny guy in a fireman's hat turn the hose on her and she danced in the spray. Her normally fresh-from-the-salon red hair hung in wet ringlets that clung to her face and shoulders. Catcalls and whistles erupted from the crowd as Claire did a seductive dance to the bass-laden music that pumped out of the speakers all around the room.

From the stage, Claire winked at her and waved. Lucy sank down a little in her chair.

"Your friend's quite the dancer."

Lucy looked up to see Judd's brother Mason standing next to her, a drink in his hand. They hadn't seen each other since that day when Judd had introduced them.

"And fearless, too," she said.

He smiled, his gaze locked on Claire for a moment. "Mind if I sit here?"

"Go right ahead. I didn't know you spent any leisure time at the resort."

"I try to attend various events, hang out at the pool or the bar now and then to make sure everything's running smoothly."

Claire's turn on stage ended to an uproar of applause and masculine exclamations of approval. She turned and gave her almost-bare rear end a shake at the crowd, then blew kisses and waved, looking as if she was having the time of her life. Lucy marveled at how different she was from her best friend.

"Was this event your idea?"

"Yeah, way back when. The first one happened years ago, and since then it's become a sort of Fantasy Ranch tradition."

Up on stage, the woman Lucy had seen at the pool party wearing nothing but cling wrap was now decked out in a bra and panties fashioned out of the same pink plastic.

"Amazing."

Mason grinned. "She's a regular at the ranch, comes at least every six months or so. The plastic wrap stuff is her trademark."

"I guess nothing surprises you, hanging around this place all the time."

"Oh, I can still be surprised now and then," he said mysteriously.

"How did you come to own the ranch?" Lucy asked, although she had a vague recollection of the story from the travel agency.

"It was a nearly bankrupt spa-type resort when I bought it ten years ago. I had a vision of a resort for singles and couples, a sort of adult playground, and lucky for me there was a big market for just this kind of place."

"You've got quite a mind for business then—this place is already legendary."

He shrugged. "The ranch has taken on a life of its own. Things sometimes get wilder here than I'd like, and it's an uphill battle to keep our reputation from becoming sleazy."

Lucy glanced around the packed bar. "I'd say you're doing fine."

Mason had achieved minor celebrity status over the years, Lucy knew. With his classic good looks and wealth, plus his bachelor status in his late thirties, he regularly made the silly Most Eligible Bachelor lists that magazines put out every year.

On stage, the auction was about to begin. Lucy was amazed that any woman would subject herself to being auctioned off in her underwear, even for a good cause, but there were at least seven women up there who'd been thrilled to do it. Claire was number five in the auction lineup.

"Is this guy bothering you?"

Lucy turned to the familiar voice and found Judd, holding a drink tray and wearing his cowboy bimbo suit again. "Not at all."

"Here to watch the festivities?" he asked Mason.

"Oh, I may even do a little bidding myself."

Judd's eyebrows shot upward. "Are you sure that's a good idea?"

"Why not? I can make a sizable donation to charity, and show one of my guests a good time for the evening."

Judd turned and surveyed the stage where the auction was going strong, already on contestant number two. "*Which* guest?"

Mason made a show of studying the remaining contestants. "I may have to do some investigating of my own tonight."

"Mason," he said in a warning tone. "Leave the investigating to me."

Lucy finally understood. "You're not thinking of buying *Claire* for the night, are you?"

But her question was drowned out by the auctioneer's voice announcing "sold" for contestant number two, a woman wearing a black leather maze of straps and buckles. Did that actually qualify as lingerie? Glancing around, she could see that no one in the audience was worried about such minor details.

"How about you get us another round of drinks, little brother?"

"How about you shove that empty glass up your—"

"And now we come to our next contestant!"

"Lucy, would you like another drink?"

"A Shirley Temple, please." She breathed a sigh of relief when Judd nodded and headed toward the bar.

"You and Judd don't get along so well, I see."

Mason grinned. "He's just got an attitude problem, that's all. I think he's still mad at me for bullying him around when we were kids."

"I think he's mad at you for making him wear that crazy outfit."

A mischievous glint appeared in his eyes. "You think?"

Lucy sighed. "I'm glad I don't have any siblings."

Mason nodded, and they watched the auction in silence. Judd dropped Lucy's drink off to her, giving Mason a warning glare the entire time, then went off to the next table, a group of women that seemed to be having a great time ogling him. Lucy watched him with a feeling of possessiveness as one woman blatantly flirted, placing her hand on his bare shoulder, laughing at a comment Lucy couldn't hear.

"Judd's got himself a fan club already, and he's only been here two weeks."

"A fan club?"

"Female guests fawning over him, slipping their room keys into his pocket, hanging out in front of his room to catch him when he's off duty." Mason shook his head. "I tell you, working here has some serious advantages for a single guy."

Lucy suddenly felt as if someone was standing on her chest. Judd had a fan club... But of course he did. He was a gorgeous man at a resort full of bold women. It just never occurred to her until now that she might not be the only woman getting Judd's special attention. Maybe the reason he seemed to be trying to avoid her lately was that he'd found someone far more interesting than Lucy to spend his nights with.

She watched him edge his way through the crowd to get back to the bar and, sure enough, all along the way women noticed him appreciatively. Of course he wasn't hers to claim, but now, without a doubt, she knew that's what she wanted.

She didn't want Judd as a partner for a few nights of casual passion. She wanted him to be hers, every night. She wanted to seduce him permanently, and she had no idea how to go about doing it.

There was no time to mull over her realization, though, because Claire had just stepped to the front of the stage to be auctioned, and Mason had grabbed a bidding sign from somewhere.

"You *are* going to bid on her!"

He shrugged. "What can I say? I'm a passionate supporter of desert wildlife preservation."

Lucy sat back in her chair and sipped her Shirley Temple, watching in fascination as the bidding for her best friend rose in a matter of minutes to two thousand dollars. By then there were only two bidders left, Mason and an elderly man in a black muscle shirt.

"I might be in trouble here," Mason said while the auctioneer spoke. "The other guy bidding is a local millionaire."

"Do I hear twenty-five hundred?" the auctioneer called.

Mason raised his sign, along with the millionaire.

Lucy leaned forward, excited by the fast bidding.

"Five thousand dollars!" the millionaire called.

The crowd gasped, and Mason smiled and raised his sign.

"Ten thousand."

"Fifteen!"

"Twenty," Mason called nonchalantly, as if he were speaking of twenty dollars, not thousands of them.

Cheers and whistles erupted from the crowd.

The auctioneer stood on stage silent, his mouth agape at the fast-rising bids. Claire, who stood next to him, simply smiled and wiggled her hips as if she fully expected to command such a high price. The crowd grew quiet as everyone looked to the elderly man for a counter bid.

He threw up his arms. "She's yours!"

"We have twenty thousand dollars. Is that our final bid?"

Silence.

"Sold! For twenty thousand dollars to our very own Fantasy Ranch owner, Mr. Mason Walker!"

The crowd cheered and hooted. Mason excused himself from the table to go claim his prize, and Lucy looked around for Judd. Across the room, he was smiling and talking to a beautiful dark-haired woman who looked vaguely like the star of a popular sitcom. She bit her lip, then tossed back the remains of her Shirley Temple and slammed the glass on the table.

"You like company?"

Before she could respond, the Russian Zorro from the pool party was taking a seat next to her. This was turning into one cruddy night.

"Actually, someone's sitting there."

"You have beautiful smile, and how do you say...lovely ass."

"Excuse me?" She glared at him. "Maybe other women here like to be talked to that way, but I prefer more tasteful—"

"Oh, no. I say wrong thing. My English is not so

good. I mean to say you have lovely eyes. It not coming out sounding that way, I see."

She smiled tightly, not sure if he was lying. "Well, thank you then."

"In my own country, I look all over for woman as beautiful as you, but I never find one."

Lucy looked around for an escape, but saw nothing promising. Across the room, Judd was still chatting with the same woman, her body language practically screaming "your place or mine." She sighed. Boring Lucy might have sat here and endured small talk with Russian Zorro, but Wild-and-Crazy Lucy had to be more proactive.

What to do, though? That was her dilemma.

"You have hair like great Russian field of wheat, and your lips are like delicious...how you say? Sausages?"

"I don't think that's the word you're looking for."

The beautiful brunette was whispering in Judd's ear. Lucy wanted to throw something at her.

"You have boyfriend, yes? He is fool to leave you alone, woman like you with such beautiful bosoms. And your legs, they are many kilometers long, like a great beautiful stork. I think you and me, we make fine children together. How 'bout it, eh?"

She had to get rid of this guy. "I should tell you, I'm suffering from a sort of...illness."

"You are sick? I make you feel better."

"Oh, no, it's not curable. I don't know what you call it in Russian, but my grandmother used to call it the nasty woman's disease."

Zorro must have understood, because he scooted back just a bit. "I'm sorry to hear this."

"You see that woman over there, talking to the waiter?" She pointed to the beautiful brunette.

"Yes. She have beautiful bosoms, too, like you."

"I happen to know for a fact that she adores foreign men. I was talking to her in the steam room the other day," Lucy lied, "and apparently she has this sort of personal goal, to make love to a man from every country in the world."

"Really? You think she find Russian man yet?"

"I don't think so, and I wouldn't be a very good friend if I didn't tell you to go over there and let her know you're available."

"Yes." He stood. "Thank you! I must go make love with her for Mother Russia."

He headed across the room, and Lucy felt the tension drain from her shoulders. Judd was no longer talking to the woman, but she didn't see him anywhere. On stage, the men's wet boxer competition was beginning.

Another guy, this one wearing a Miami Vice-era pink blazer, was heading straight for Lucy when Claire and Mason showed up.

"Good timing, you guys. I was about to ward off a Don Johnson wannabe."

"You're supposed to be here flirting, not scaring everyone away," Claire said.

Mason smiled. "We're leaving. Will you be okay here alone? We can stay if you'd prefer."

"No, Lucy needs to overcome her wallflower tendencies. That's why I sent her here."

But she'd already met a guy, and now none of the others would do. "Go ahead. I'm perfecting my comebacks to sleazy pick-up lines."

Mason gave Claire a speculative look. "You might learn something from Lucy, you know. A little reservation can be a good thing."

Claire crossed her arms over her damp, bustier-clad chest. "What do you know? You just spent twenty-thousand dollars to go on a date with me. It smacks of desperation, if you ask me."

Lucy's jaw dropped. "Claire!"

"Just kidding."

"No, she wasn't, but that's okay. We've got the whole night ahead of us to figure each other out."

They left the bar, Claire leading the way. Lucy felt bad for Mason. Claire hadn't met a man yet that she believed was worthy of her. She used them for her purposes and then got rid of them like last season's shoes.

Turning her attention back to the stage, Lucy did a double take. The lights in the Idle Spurs Lounge might have been dim, but there was no mistaking the man on stage in nothing but a pair of black silk boxers.

It was Judd.

 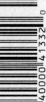

# Vlasic Tastes Best

Agree or It's Free*

Bread & Butter Chips
MILDLY SWEET & SPICY

Kosher D
CLASSIC D

# Why Buy Any

...t of the speakers on
...r next contestant. He's
...color is red and his fa-
...ts you... It's Judd!"

...age wearing a red bikini
... water hose on Judd and
... A roar went up in the
...s, clapped, screamed. Al-
though he didn't look to be having nearly as good a
time as the other wet and soon-to-be wet men on the
stage, he smiled like a good sport and did the required
dance across stage and back.

Lucy gripped the table and tried not to fall out of
her chair. He was even sexier wet than he was dry,
and wet boxers or not, he had the best-looking rear
end she'd ever seen. Apparently all the women in the
audience agreed with her. Several pairs of panties
flew through the air and landed on stage at his feet,
leaving Lucy to wonder how anyone could remove
their underpants so fast.

And then she realized that Judd would soon be up
for auction. Her guy was about to be bought by another woman! She couldn't let it happen. This was her
chance to get him all to herself for an entire evening
before her vacation ended, no investigation to worry

about, no Claire to interrupt them, and she was going to take it.

Four other men were ahead of Judd in line for the bidding, so she waited patiently as women placed their bids and won. Then it was Judd's turn, and as he stepped to the front of the stage, she felt sweat beading on her forehead. What if she couldn't bid fast enough? What if she couldn't bid high enough?

All around her women were waiting with their bidding signs poised, ready to claim Judd for their own. She couldn't let it happen. Doing a mental count, she totaled the money she had in checking and savings combined. The bidding was for charity, so it was okay to spend whatever it took to get him.

She deserved it. The desert wildlife deserved it.

"Bidding starts at one hundred dollars. Can we get a hundred bucks for this fine male specimen named Judd?"

All around the room signs shot up, including Lucy's, and before she had time to take a breath the bidding had risen to three hundred. Judd searched the audience until he found her sitting there alone at the table. He gave her a silent nod and a smile.

Quite a few bidders dropped out after three hundred, but Lucy and four other very determined women hung in there. At six hundred, two more bidders dropped out, and Lucy got a queasy feeling as she wondered exactly how high she'd have to go to get her man. She did a second count of the extra money in her savings account and decided, What the heck?

"One thousand dollars!" she called.

Judd's eyes widened and several audience members gasped.

"We've got one thousand dollars here for a guy that really knows how to please a woman. Can we get eleven hundred? He's a catch, ladies. Do I hear eleven hundred?"

Her competing bidders shook their heads, and with that the announcer called, "Sold, to the pretty lady in the red dress!"

Her heart rate slowed, and people around her called congratulations. She'd done it! She'd bought herself a whole night with the man of her fantasies.


"YOU SHOULDN'T HAVE SPENT all that money." Judd was flattered, but he had every intention of splitting the cost of the donation with her. Whether she wanted him to or not.

"It's for a good cause."

"You could have just asked me for a date and gotten it free."

"Oh, really? When you've been spending most of your waking hours trying to avoid me these past few days?"

"I have not."

"You have! You don't want my help with the investigation, and you act a little freaked out every time we kiss."

She was right, he did feel off kilter every time they kissed, but that was only because of the incredible heat those kisses generated, only because he knew how lost he could get with Lucy.

Tonight was a perfect example. There he'd been up

on stage feeling like a complete fool, and then he saw her bidding on him and all his embarrassment melted away. He got so lost in thoughts of having a night alone with Lucy that he'd nearly forgotten he was standing on a stage soaking wet in nothing but his underwear.

Maybe he'd gotten a little annoyed at times that she was butting in on his investigation, but only because she distracted him so much that after a few hours with her, he didn't care one iota about who was trying to ruin his brother's business.

"So you admit that you don't want me around."

"Not exactly."

"Then you're saying you do want me around?"

"Not exactly."

"What then?"

"Oh, I definitely want you around tonight. I can think of all kinds of reasons why you should be here right now, with me and no one else."

"Really?" A little smile played on her lips.

"Sure."

"What sorts of reasons?"

"How about we finish this discussion later? If we don't get going we're gonna miss our reservation."

Although Lucy's bid for Judd was high, it was only the third highest of the night. Judd didn't feel too insulted for not having commanded the highest price, especially since the guy who'd won momentarily pulled down his boxers on stage. He felt guilty that Lucy thought she needed to spend any money at all to be with him.

After Judd went backstage to get dressed, they

made their way to the resort's main restaurant. He intended for them to have a late dinner before taking a walk, maybe catching the live performance of the Wild, Wild West Show. He couldn't let himself think too much about what might happen after that, when they were alone together and the night was theirs. If he did, he'd have to skip dinner and all the rest and take Lucy straight to bed.

They had dinner outside on the restaurant patio, with a desert breeze cooling the night air. Lucy looked incredible, and he could tell by her slightly giddy mood that she was anticipating tonight's events as much as he was. By the time they arrived at the Wild, Wild West Show, the air between them was alive with electricity.

Memories of what happened while they'd watched the show's rehearsal made Judd restless in his seat. Lucy must have understood what all his shifting and fidgeting was about.

She leaned forward and whispered into his ear just as the curtains on stage began to open. "One time watching the half-naked cowboys and bar girls dancing around and singing was enough for me."

"You sure?"

"Let's get out of here."

In a matter of minutes they were back at Judd's room. As he searched for the keys to the door, a couple passed by.

"Hey, it's you, my friend!" the man said to Lucy in a heavy Russian accent. "You do me big favor. Thank you!" He gave his companion's shoulder a suggestive squeeze.

Judd recognized the Russian's date as the same woman who'd been hitting on him earlier in the lounge. He'd finally had to lie and tell her he was engaged to another woman to get away from her.

She eyed Lucy, then Judd. "Your fiancée?"

Judd grinned. "Yep, this is her."

Lucy frowned at Judd but said nothing, and the Russian man looked at her as if he wanted to speak, but didn't.

Why did calling Lucy his fiancée feel so comfortable? She wasn't the kind of woman he needed at all. Yet she was exactly what he wanted. That was Judd's problem, always wanting the wrong kind of woman.

Instead of being drawn to steady, sensible types, he chased after women who set his blood boiling, women who rendered him unable to think straight. Invariably those women were unreliable, flaky and ruled by their passions. And also invariably, Judd got burned.

Inside the room Lucy asked, "I'm your fiancée?"

"It was the only way to get rid of her. What is this favor you did for her friend?"

She gave him a secretive smile. "I did a little lying of my own to get rid of him earlier."

"That guy was hitting on you?"

"Does that surprise you? He compared my lips to sausages."

*Sausages?* "You're lucky you don't have every guy at the resort lined up to whisper bad metaphors in your ear."

"Right." Lucy rolled her eyes and flopped down onto the bed, reminding Judd of what they should have been doing instead of talking.

He sat on the nearest chair and tugged off one of his boots.

"Seriously, men are intimidated by you," he said, but "you" came out a sort of grunt as he gave his other boot a tug.

When Lucy didn't respond, he looked up to see a baffled expression on her face. "What, men think I'm going to beat them up?"

He suppressed a grin. "I mean, intimidated by your looks."

She blinked, incomprehension in her eyes. "You've got to be kidding."

"Why do you think every single male guest at the ranch doesn't follow you around throwing their room numbers at you?"

Her cheeks took on a pretty pink tone. "Why?"

"Because you're too attractive and aloof. Men like to hit on women they think they'll have a chance with. There's just the occasional nutcase like me—and Mr. Russia out there—who isn't intimidated by the staggering odds against him."

She giggled. "Don't forget Speedo Man."

"Yeah, him, too."

"All this false flattery is unnecessary, you know. You've already got me in your room."

Someone needed to set Lucy straight, once and for all. Where she got such a distorted self-image, he had no idea, but she deserved to know the truth. And besides, if he didn't take his time, he'd fumble through the night too fast, like a virgin schoolboy.

He went to her and took her by the arm, then led her to the dresser mirror. "Now, look here."

She glared at his reflection.

"Look at yourself." He stood behind her, and the fruity scent of her shampoo gave him the urge to press his hips against her behind, slide his hands around her waist, and—

*Whoa, boy.*

"What you see here is a beautiful woman. The kind of woman who has a lot of power over men, whether she realizes it or not."

"Look, I know I'm not hideous, but I really don't believe—"

"Hideous?" He tried not to smile. "I'm the guy here. I get to decide how attractive you are."

One pointy elbow shot back and nailed him in the ribs. Lucy's eyes had narrowed and she was poised to strike again.

"Ouch! Okay, that probably sounded pretty pigheaded, but you have an unrealistic self-image."

She let her arm fall to her side again, but made no comment.

"Now, let's start with one of your best features, your hair. See how it falls around your face and into your eyes sometimes? That's sexy. And these curls that make you look like you just crawled out of bed? Those are really sexy."

She was blushing again. "Judd, this isn't necessary." She tried to move out of his grasp, but he held her there.

In her movement she brushed her rear end against his pelvis, and his whole body tensed. His voice tight, he said, "Yes, it is."

Lucy stilled. A look of comprehension came over

her face, and slowly she pressed herself into him again. "Are you trying to drag this out?"

Her voice was low and breathy enough to drive a man insane with desire. Judd willed himself to be patient.

"Now, let's move on to your eyes. Nature should never have produced such a warm shade of brown, because on you it has the power to make men slobbering imbeciles. But it's not just the color, it's the way your use your eyes, looking straight at people when you talk to them, cutting your gaze away when you're embarrassed. Very sexy."

She made a little sound of disbelief, but he could tell by those revealing eyes of hers that she was starting to enjoy this. And that she had a game of her own in mind. She squirmed against him, closely watching his reaction in the mirror, looking pleased when he let out a gasp.

Judd pressed his eyes shut tight and thought about doing his taxes, changing the oil in his car—anything but Lucy.

"Brown eyes are boring."

"No, far from it, but let's move on. We've still got a lot to cover. Your mouth is definitely one of your better features. I mean, when you chew on your lip, or smile, or wet your lips with your tongue—those are the kinds of things that drive men wild."

She studied her mouth closely, as if seeing it for the first time. "Really?"

He felt her arms and shoulders relax, and it took all his willpower not to sink into her and let their bodies melt together. "Yeah, really," he said, but his voice came out sounding strangled.

She looked pleased.

But he couldn't help noticing the way she tensed when he put his hands on her waist, the way she closed her eyes for a moment as if to revel in the tension between them, the way her lips parted slightly and her breath quickened. She felt it, too. He was treading on dangerous ground, but he couldn't turn back.

"Let's don't forget your nose. Normally, I don't notice a woman's nose unless there's something odd about it, but yours manages to be pretty sexy. It's straight, but not too long, the perfect size for your face, and when you get angry and you do that little nostril flaring thing... That's *really* sexy."

She frowned. "I flare my nostrils?"

"Yes, you do. But we've still got a lot to cover.

"Some men don't notice necks, but yours is pretty noticeable, especially when you pull your hair up. It's long and straight and made for kissing, and it leads down to a very beautiful pair of shoulders." He lifted one hand to trail along one shoulder bone. "These shoulders were meant to go bare. It's a crime to cover them up in long-sleeved shirts."

Lucy squirmed, her hips brushed his groin, and the sensation was enough to make him forget his resolve and take her right there, bent over the dresser, in front of the mirror so he could see her face as he thrust into her.

"But then, the same could be said of your breasts. Perfect size, perfect shape, it's a shame to cover them."

It was a mistake to look in the mirror at that little hint of cleavage peaking out from her neckline. When he saw it, he knew he had to touch her there. And then he remembered how perfect her breasts had felt in his mouth, and how much she'd loved being kissed there, and he couldn't stop his hands from sliding down, from tracing the lower half of her breasts with his fingertips until her breath quickened and his erection threatened to wear a hole in the front of his jeans.

Once his hands had made it that far, they couldn't *not* go further. He let his fingers move up to trace the indention of her cleavage.

Lucy's breath was coming out ragged now, as was his. The slight smile she wore suggested she knew she'd won the game. Her eyes closed, she let her head fall back and to the side, exposing a delicious expanse of neck Judd couldn't resist tasting. He gave in, lowered his lips and brushed them against her lightly, and then more forcefully when she let out a little sigh of pleasure.

She slid her hand behind her back, between them, and gripped him lightly, just enough to drive him insane. He reached down and stopped her.

With one hand he clasped her wrists together and held them in front of her, while with his other hand he pulled her dress up until it was gathered around her waist, revealing a barely there pair of black lace panties that looked as if they could be ripped off with one good tug.

He brought his mouth down next to her ear again and whispered, "Have you ever watched yourself make love?"

For such a little vixen, she sure could embarrass easily. Her cheeks colored and her eyes widened for a moment, but she simply shook her head no.

"I want you to watch."

Judd couldn't remember wanting anything so badly as he wanted to drive himself into her right at that moment, but if didn't practice a little restraint, he'd be finished in world-record time. So he pulled her dress the rest of the way off and undid her bra, then freed her of her panties.

It was all too much for Judd. When he spoke again, his voice was barely above a whisper. "You have these perfectly round hips that men just can't help imagining the feel of." He slid his hands down the slight hourglass shape of her figure. "The kind of hips made for holding on to..."

He lowered his lips and again brushed them against her neck lightly. She tasted like heaven.

With his penis straining against her, he wasn't quite sure he could make it the rest of the way through his lesson unless he hurried—*really hurried*. He stopped the kiss.

Willing some measure of control into his voice, he whispered in her ear, "One of your best features is your legs. They're not too skinny, but shapely enough to show that you must exercise. And men, being the sexual creatures we are, can't help but imagine how those long gorgeous legs would feel wrapped around us—"

When he lowered himself onto his knees and spread her legs apart, she made a little sound of protest, but he held her in place and stopped for a moment to admire every naked inch of her. He hadn't lied—she was gorgeous in the most irresistible sort of way.

He slid his hands up her inner thighs and let his fingers explore for a moment. She was already wet and ready for him, very wet. He intended to make her even wetter.

Grasping her hips, he guided her into a more tilted position and slid his tongue inside her. She cried out, and he felt a burst of possessiveness fill his chest. He was the first to do this to her, he suspected, amazing as it seemed. And if he had his way, he'd make sure she never forgot how it felt to be loved by him.

But she barely gave him a chance to practice one of his favorite arts, because as he let his tongue explore, her body tensed and her muscles contracted in release, and she made ragged moaning sounds as he held her and kissed her inner thigh.

Judd's every nerve was alive with the sexual tension that hung in the air, and he felt like he did the first time he'd ever made love—as if he were about to be a changed man, as if this one event was going to shape him in ways he couldn't yet imagine.

If he hadn't been so damned hot with desire, he might have been scared out of his wits. That was just too much to contemplate at the moment.

It only took a minute for him to rid himself of his clothes with Lucy's help. But then her gaze darted back and forth between him and the boots he'd discarded earlier on the floor.

"Um, I was wondering if you'd mind…" Her cheeks colored, but she met his gaze. "If you'd mind wearing the boots."

"Right now?"

She dug her toe into the carpet and twisted it around. "I've always had this fantasy about making love to a cowboy in nothing but his boots."

Judd couldn't refuse a request like that. He retrieved the boots and put them back on. Then, feeling only slightly ridiculous, he went to her and picked up a condom from the dresser.

Shyly she reached for it. "Allow me," she whispered.

As Lucy slid the condom over his rigid erection, Judd feared his legs would give out. Her fingers brushed against him, first tentatively, then with more confidence, but he couldn't take the sweet torture.

He reached down and stopped her. "Honey, I'll be finished before we even get started."

Lucy slid her arms around his neck to kiss him, but he turned her back around and kissed her from behind.

"I want you to watch, remember?"

"But—"

He silenced her with another kiss and she didn't protest, instead turning her head and lifting herself up on tiptoes to reach him better. She reached up and plunged her fingers into his hair, pulled him closer.

He couldn't hold out another second. Breaking the kiss, he guided her forward and bent his knees to accommodate her shorter height, and slid into her.

Lucy gasped, watching him in the mirror as he began to move inside her. She'd forgotten all her inhibitions by now, he figured, and they could both feel nothing but how perfectly their bodies worked together. Then she arched her back, leaned her head back, let her lips part as she gasped, and Judd was nearly lost.

He needed her closer, pressed against him. So with all his willpower he managed to stop the building momentum long enough to turn her around and rest her bottom on the top of the dresser. She wrapped her legs around his waist and he entered her again, this time on the very edge of climax.

But no, he couldn't just yet. He wanted to be sure they came together. He dipped his head down to taste her breasts, and she moaned. He teased and sucked and caressed, and her body grew tenser by the second.

"Please, Judd... Please."

He slid deep into her again, and again, finding a rhythm that was completely out of his control, a force created by their two bodies.

He was lost.

He gripped her hips for dear life as their bodies released together. He held her close, pressed his face into her shoulder, tried not to think about the emotion that filled his chest in that moment. He didn't want to acknowledge it, didn't want to name it, didn't want to admit what dangerous territory he'd entered.

Judd carried Lucy to bed and stretched out beside her so they could rest up for the next round.

## 11

SHE WAS RUINED for any other man. Ruined, ruined, ruined. It was sad, really. Who could hope to compare to a man like Judd?

Lucy's past sexual experiences included one boyfriend who actually wrote their planned sexual encounters into his day planner, complete with a beginning and ending time, and another whose idea of wild sex was doing it with the TV on. He liked to watch CNN during their lovemaking, claiming it helped him last longer. Lucy suspected it had more to do with his crush on a certain female news anchor.

Her experience might have been limited, and probably not very interesting, but she knew for certain that she'd found the best with Judd. He understood her body in ways not even she did, and he used that knowledge well.

*Quite* well.

He'd made love to her four times in a row, but she'd lost count of the number of orgasms she'd had. Possibly enough to last her a lifetime, since she surely wasn't going to find another guy like Judd anytime soon—perhaps ever.

And he knew how to charm. That whole speech about her attractive features was all part of his skill as a lover, she figured. He must have understood how much psychology played into a woman's enjoyment of sex, and he'd simply obliged her. But none of it could be very true. She knew she wasn't unattractive with her new look, but she certainly was no goddess, the way Judd made her out to be.

It was sweet of him to claim that men didn't approach her because they were intimidated, but it just plain wasn't true. Still, she adored him for saying it.

Not only did she adore his charm, she loved everything about him. She loved his commitment to his work, his sense of humor... She loved *him*. Heaven help her, she did. She'd gone and foolishly fallen in love with the guy she was supposed to be using for a week of meaningless sex.

She stared at the ceiling, amazed by her realization. How could she have let this happen? How could she be so stupid? And the worst part of all was that he couldn't possibly love her back—not the real her, anyway. The only Lucy that Judd knew was the one she pretended to be, the wild risk-taker with the sexy wardrobe. Everything he liked about her wasn't even part of the real, boring her.

She couldn't let such depressing thoughts ruin a perfectly wonderful moment, though. Here she was, lying naked with the man of her fantasies, and she was going to enjoy it while it lasted.

Lucy rolled over and let her gaze travel down the full length of him sleeping beside her. He hadn't bothered to pull any covers over himself, and he was there in all his naked glory for her to admire.

Well, except for those cowboy boots. She tried to

suppress a giggle, but it slipped out anyway, waking Judd.

He stretched and groaned. "Were you just giggling?"

"Sorry, I thought of something funny, that's all." But her gaze betrayed her by straying back to his boots.

Sure, he looked sexy in them—he could look sexy in a polyester leisure suit—but it was the thought that he hadn't bothered to take off the boots even after they'd retired to the bed that really sent her into a fit of giggles. He'd slept in them all night long.

"Are you laughing at my boots?" He sounded more amused than annoyed.

She fell back on the bed and giggled until it hurt.

"You are!"

"Not exactly." She gasped for breath. "Well, yeah, I guess I am." And that sent her into another peal of laughter.

Before she could protest, Judd was up and straddling her, pinning her to the bed. "Let me give you a tip—never giggle at a naked man if you care at all for his psychological well-being."

"I'm sorry."

He suppressed a smile. "You've hurt my feelings. I don't know if I can accept an apology just yet."

"I hope you realize that no sane woman would giggle at *you* for the reason most men fear."

"Is that so?" He raised one suspicious eyebrow.

She let her gaze fall below his waistline. "Definitely. Now what can I do to make you feel better?"

He gave her a dangerous smile as he leaned forward and pinned her hands at her sides. "You can help me get these boots off."

A few moments later, with several good tugs, she'd removed his boots.

"What's on the investigation agenda for today?" Lucy asked.

"Tomorrow is the big day for the end-of-summer celebration. If I don't find some proof that Buck's behind the sabotage, who knows what might go wrong."

"Does that mean you're finally admitting that I'm right, that Claire has nothing to do with it?"

He grinned. "I'll leave that for Mason to find out, if he hasn't already. Claire's a dead end for me right now. I think Buck is the key to solving this case."

"But if it isn't Buck, something could go wrong either way."

Judd exhaled. "He's our most likely suspect—disgruntled employee with a history of blowups at management. I've got a hunch about him, and my hunches are never wrong."

"Oh, yeah? Did you have a hunch about me?"

He let his gaze slide over the length of her. "I had a hunch you'd be my downfall, and I was right."

Lucy smiled. Now that she'd lived out her cowboy fantasy, she was feeling bold. So far Judd had mostly taken the lead in their lovemaking. She wanted to try out her own newfound courage.

"I'm going to take a shower. Care to join me?"

Judd's eyes perked up. "See what I mean? That's a wicked invitation I can't turn down."

Amazed at her own boldness, Lucy strolled across the sunlit room naked, not even feeling shy about her state of undress. She went into the bathroom and turned on the water, then poked her head out and motioned for Judd to follow.

He came into the bathroom and stopped, letting his gaze travel over her slowly from head to toe as she stood poised next to the shower. "You look exquisite."

Lucy blushed, feeling shy all over again. "Flattery is unnecessary. You've already gotten me into bed."

"You're the strangest woman. Modest to a fault."

She started to protest, but then reminded herself to say the opposite of what the old Lucy might say. "It's one of my charms."

"Yeah, that it is," he conceded with a little smile.

Lucy turned and checked the water temperature, blinking back a sudden dampness in her eyes. How on earth was she ever going to go back to living a normal life, a life without Judd, in only two more days?

She'd just have to make the most of this short time with him, and she could think of no better way to do it than in the shower. She hopped in and squealed at the assault of the water on her barely awake body.

"Water's perfect, come on in!"

Judd pulled aside the sliding-glass door and stepped in, then closed it behind him. He flinched and jumped back when the water hit him.

"Yow, woman! You like it hot, don't you?"

Lucy pushed the water off her face and smiled. "Water's not the only thing I like hot."

She pulled him close and gave him a kiss that let him know she wanted control this time. For Judd's part, he seemed more than happy to oblige. When she took the bar of soap and began lathering him up, he raised his arms, tilted his head back, and closed his eyes, seeming to savor her every touch.

Her confidence bolstered all the more, Lucy ran her hands over every inch of his torso, letting the water splash the suds off as soon as she created them. She turned him around and took her time washing his back, pressing her fingers into his flesh to massage as she worked.

This—showering with a man, washing him, sharing such a mundane chore—was the sort of thing Lucy had imagined doing with her husband someday. If only Judd could be the man she shared her life with...

Whoa.

Where the heck had that crazy thought come from? She'd apparently taken her confidence and dived into the deep end with it. Lucy forced her thoughts back to the realistic, the here and now. Maybe her deceit kept her from any kind of future with Judd, but it couldn't keep her from enjoying the present.

She let her hands drop to Judd's buttocks, then down to his thighs, his calves, and back up. She turned him around again and trailed kisses up his bulging thigh muscle. When she came to his erection, she knelt in front of him. She washed him slowly, letting her fingers memorize his every contour, watching the slick suds wash away in the spray of the shower.

And then she took him into her mouth an inch at a time.

Judd gasped. One hand steadied him against the tile wall and the other dropped down to gently cup Lucy's head. His body quivered in her grasp.

This was power. And oh, how she loved it.

She savored the taste of him, the feel of his straining body, the intimate rhythm they found together. She'd dared to have such fantasies in her most private moments, but she'd never imagined the real thing would be so good.

Judd finally tugged at her, urging her to rise. "I want to be inside you," he whispered.

But Lucy wasn't ready for it to end. Not quite yet.

She stood and handed Judd the bar of soap. "I haven't gotten my bath yet. Would you mind?"

Judd let out a ragged breath and smiled at her game. "Oh, you want to play the tease, do you?"

Lucy shrugged, feigning innocence.

He rubbed the soap between his hands and stroked one of her breasts. "We'll just have to see who cries uncle first."

JUDD SPOTTED BUCK rounding the corner of the building, heading toward the resort entrance. When he stopped at the payphone, Judd ducked behind a line of bushes and slowly made his way closer until he was within listening distance. He barely had the strength to crouch in the bushes, thanks to his all-night marathon with Lucy, and after a minute his leg muscles began to tremble. Judd couldn't remember ever having had so much mind-blowing sex in one night.

A middle-aged couple wearing matching gold lamé swimsuits passed by and gave Judd strange looks, but made no comment.

"Yeah, everything's set up, so when do you want it to happen?" He heard Buck saying.

Aha.

"Right, uh-huh. I'll call you back after and let you know if it goes as planned." A pause. "Yeah, I know. I didn't forget. I'll do my best." He hung up the phone and stamped his cigarette on the ground.

Bingo.

Something was about to go down again, and it sounded as if Buck was going to be the one to make it happen. But who had he been talking to? Who was giving him the instructions?

He'd tried talking to other employees about Buck, digging for gossip, but all the gossip revolved around his sexual exploits. Men admired Buck and women were attracted to him. No one seemed to dislike him, and no one would say anything negative about him. His blowups with management were legendary, but everyone wrote them off as a side effect of his short temper. They simply added to Buck's mystique.

"There you are!"

Judd nearly lost his balance leaning against the wood fence at the unexpected sound of Lucy's voice.

"Shh!"

"Oh, sorry. Did I interrupt something?" she said in a whisper, looking around for a reason to be quiet.

"Not now. I just caught a phone conversation that might be important."

Her eyes lit up. "Buck?"

"Yep. I think something's about to happen, so we have to either stop it before it does, or be there to clean up the mess."

"Shouldn't we be following him?"

"*I* should be. That's what I was about to do when you popped up."

"Let's go before he gets away." Lucy took off in the direction of Buck, who was quickly disappearing in the distance, headed toward the employee rooms.

"Lucy, wait a minute. Why don't you let me handle this now? You've been a great help, but we have no idea if there's any danger involved here."

She turned and glared at him. "If you really thought I was a great help, you'd let me help now. You think I'm a pain in the rear, don't you?"

In ways she couldn't begin to imagine.

He stifled a grin. "You said it, not me."

She made a show of looking offended. "Jerk."

Up ahead, Buck entered a building and Judd quickened his pace. "If you've got to tag along, try to be quiet."

"Fine."

She wasn't exactly dressed for detective work, in her little flowery summer dress and strappy high-heeled sandals, but she was easy on the eyes, so he couldn't complain. Actually, although he didn't plan on admitting it to her, she was a pretty helpful assistant, during those times when she wasn't making him forget his own name.

By the time they reached the employee residence building, Buck was nowhere to be seen. A quick listen at his door revealed that he was inside, and it sounded as though he was getting ready for a shower.

"What do you hear?" Lucy whispered a little too loudly.

"Shh." He held up a finger telling her to wait as he listened again. "Just running water."

"That means we could sneak into his room while

he's in there, see if there's any indication of what his plans are."

Judd resisted the urge to point out that he'd already thought of that, and he slowly tested the doorknob. It was locked.

"Just use the management's master key set," Lucy whispered, echoing his thoughts again.

He dug into his pocket and found it empty. Oops. "Um, I'm not sure where they are."

Footsteps around the corner sent them scurrying away from Buck's door. They pretended to be casually strolling down the hallway, headed for Judd's room.

"I have an idea."

"I'm afraid to hear it."

"Fine, I'll just keep it to myself, and we'll never know what secrets are locked away in that room."

"Okay, I'm sorry. Please tell me your brilliant idea."

"That's better." She beamed. "You could boost me up onto his balcony and I could get into the room through the sliding doors while he's still in the shower."

"That's an awful idea. First, there's not enough time, and second, you don't even know if the sliding doors are unlocked."

She grabbed his hand and pulled him toward the exit. "I can slip in and slip back out quickly, and I saw his sliding doors standing open on our way into the building. See, I'm a pretty good detective."

It was a recipe for disaster. "If he catches you in there, what are you going to do?"

"Distract him with my feminine charms?"

"You're not going up there."

"I won't get caught!"

Outside, Judd eyed the distance between the ground and Buck's balcony and decided that if he had to catch Lucy on her way down, they'd probably survive. Lucy saw his expression and shook her head.

"Don't worry, I climbed a tree once as a kid. Just give me a boost up and I'll be fine."

"Once? What a daredevil. Did the fire department have to come and get you down?"

"Come on."

Judd sighed and admitted defeat to himself. "You're gonna have to balance on my shoulders, Spiderwoman."

"Then hush and bend over." She was taking off her sandals.

"Now those are the words I've been waiting to hear from a woman."

Lucy's knees dug into his back and she wobbled a little before making her way to his shoulders. Once there, she could reach the bottom edge of the balcony. Holding on to it for balance, she eased up onto her feet.

Judd couldn't help admiring the view as he held her feet steady. Under her dress she wore a pair of white satin panties.

"Funny, I thought you were more of a black lace kind of girl."

She let out a little gasp and gave him a swift kick in the side of the head with her foot before pulling up onto the balcony. A moment later she disappeared into the room, leaving Judd alone to contemplate his erection.

LUCY'S FACE was still burning. She hadn't thought about having to show Judd her least attractive side to get into Buck's room. But now she was here, and Buck was singing a bad rendition of a Van Halen hit in the shower.

She did a quick survey of her surroundings. Clothes were strewn around on the floor and unmade bed, a grease-stained pizza box sat on the small kitchenette table and the TV was tuned in to a music video station with the sound turned down low.

Now what? She was, after all, an amateur sleuth so she wasn't sure what to look for. What would Nancy Drew do now?

Across the room she spotted a pile of papers, but they yielded nothing more interesting than a credit card statement and some junk mail. She rummaged through his desk drawers and his dresser, but there was only the typical single-guy stuff.

She tiptoed into his kitchenette and looked through the cabinets, but found nothing more interesting than a half-empty bottle of tequila.

With Buck still singing away in the shower, she felt comfortable doing some more searching, but then the phone rang. Lucy froze in place and her heart pounded. It rang once, twice, three times. Buck must not have heard it, because he continued to sing. The answering machine picked up.

"You have reached the phone number of Buck Samson. If you are a beautiful woman, please leave your name and number and I will be happy to return your call."

*Beeeep.*

"Buck, it's me, Natasha. I know I shouldn't be calling your room line, but I forgot to tell you when you called, those things you need to complete the job? I'm having them delivered to your room at five o'clock today, so be there."

Lucy couldn't believe her luck. She'd just gathered enough information in a few minutes to nearly wrap up Judd's case! But she had to erase that message.

She hurried over to the machine. Buck's singing stopped, and the sound of running water disappeared. Lucy had to get out. No time to dawdle. Grabbing the answering machine, she yanked the cord out of the wall and tucked the machine under her arm. With any luck, he wouldn't miss it right away.

He must have dried off in record time, because before she could make it to the door, she heard him push the bathroom door open. She ran to the balcony, tossed the answering machine over the side, realizing too late that it might hit Judd.

Seconds later she'd gotten both legs over the railing; she could hear Buck in his room now. Praying Judd was there to catch her and not knocked out cold by the answering machine, she lowered herself, squatted on the outer ledge, grabbed it, and then lowered her legs.

Her arm strength had been compromised by the climb up onto the balcony, though, so instead of dangling as she'd hoped, Lucy lost her grasp and fell like a dead weight.

"Ummmph!" she heard from beneath her as she landed.

"Oh, dear! Are you okay?" She rolled off of Judd, who was now sprawled on the ground covered in desert dust. "Judd? Can you hear me?"

He opened one eye, then the other, and glared at her. "You could have told me you were going to jump!"

"Shh!" She scrambled up off the ground and tugged at his arm. "Come on, if you don't have any broken limbs we've got to get out of here."

"What about that projectile you threw at my head?"

"The answering machine—get it!"

Lucy headed around the corner of the building, where Buck couldn't see them if he looked from his balcony. Judd followed, cursing and limping. When they'd made it safely to the rear entrance, Lucy grabbed his hand and pulled him inside.

"Let's go to your room where I can tell you what happened in private."

"This better be a good story."

Lucy tugged his arm as they climbed the flight of stairs.

"I think you broke some of my ribs."

"I'll make it up to you later," she said, giddy from her adventure.

Judd unlocked his door and followed Lucy into his room. "You've got a twig in your hair." He reached up and plucked it out.

She smiled, feeling mischievous. "You've got dirt all over your shirt. You'd better take it off."

"I'd better check and make sure those pretty white panties of yours didn't get dirty, too." He lifted the edge of her dress, and she slapped him away.

"You've had more than enough time to look at my underwear today. Shame on you, taking advantage of me when I was only trying to help you solve this case."

Judd peeled his T-shirt off to reveal that chest she'd so quickly come to love. She inspected the damage, or more accurately, the lack of it. His back was a little red where he'd hit the ground, but other than that, he was perfectly, beautifully intact.

"What can I say? I'm a guy, you're a pretty girl." His expression turned serious.

"You look fine, and I've got some good stuff here," she said as she took the answering machine from him. "Let's get this thing plugged in."

Once they'd listened to the message, Judd's mood lightened considerably.

"Natasha and Buck are working together... So that's his connection to all this. And the fact that he's had some major fights with management just makes him all the more motivated to get even with the ranch."

"I understand the Fantasy Ranch is the Oasis Spa and Resort's biggest competitor, but that just doesn't seem like enough reason to me for Natasha Kendrick to try to ruin Mason's business."

"Mason and Natasha had a hot-and-heavy relationship going for a while, followed by a nasty breakup."

"Nasty enough to ruin the Fantasy Ranch?"

"She tried to burn down his house a few weeks after they broke up."

"Sounds like Mason is pretty unlucky in love. Did he deserve to have his house torched?"

Judd grinned, and Lucy resisted the urge to pounce on him.

"I wish I could say he did, but no. I'd guess the arson charges were enough to teach her to be subtle in her next act of revenge."

"So she attacks his wallet, where it hurts most."

"Exactly."

Lucy frowned. "I wonder how she got Buck to go along with her plan."

"Could be that they're lovers. Maybe Natasha heard about Buck being disgruntled when she was dating Mason. She might have been able to buy him for the right price."

Lucy bit her lip, flopped down onto the edge of Judd's bed, her mind still racing. "But I still don't get how there's a connection between any of the travel agents at Sunny Horizons and this whole mess."

"Darren Ullrich was staying here when the thefts occurred, and I'd be willing to bet money he's fooled around with Natasha, too. She would have put him up to causing some trouble here at the ranch."

"That woman gets around. Do you think Darren was the only agent involved?"

"It's hard to say. Given how Natasha works, it's possible the other male employee at your office was in on it, too."

"Frank Wiley?"

"He was staying here when the reservations disappeared from the computer system."

"He is a bit of a computer geek. And that picture we saw! He was talking to Buck!"

"Exactly. He couldn't have gotten access to the system without Buck's help."

"What about the delivery Buck's supposed to get today?"

"I'll make sure the delivery person is intercepted at the front gate, and we'll find out what it is."

Lucy flopped back onto his bed, smiling. This private eye stuff was pretty fun. "I practically solved this case for you. I think I deserve some appreciation here."

Judd stood beside the bed, peering down at her. "You'd better let me recover from my injuries before you start looking for any appreciation."

"Oh, right, your *injuries*."

He knelt beside her and moaned in mock discomfort. "I could use a little T.L.C."

Lucy smiled. "Just point to where it hurts, and I'll see what I can do."

He pointed to his left shoulder, and she placed a soft kiss there. He grunted and motioned toward his rib cage, and Lucy ran her tongue along one rib, inhaling his scent, becoming intoxicated by it.

"I'd better lie down," he said, smiling. "This is gonna take a while."

# 12

INTERCEPTING the delivery truck had been easy, but getting the delivery guy to give up the box meant for Buck should have been a challenge. Instead, Judd had simply claimed he was Buck Samson, and the man handed the box right over to him. Inside the box, he found enough ammonia and sulfur—the classic ingredients for a stink bomb—to make a stink so big it would clear out the entire resort.

"Lucky thing you caught that stuff," Mason said, peering at the box. "I think this is grounds enough to call Buck in and question him."

"You ought to go ahead and fire him. We've got that answering machine tape."

"Which you acquired by breaking into his room. Do you think there's anything else planned for tomorrow that we haven't caught?"

"Sounds like a question to ask Buck himself."

"I've already tried to find him. He's disappeared. Guess he saw his missing answering machine, figured someone was on to him."

"You think he'll come back to try to pull anything tomorrow?"

"We'd better keep an eye out, in case he does. I've got several employees looking around for him now, but I think he's left the premises."

"What about Claire? Do you think he'd try to get in touch with her?"

Mason's jaw flexed at the mention of her name. "I don't know why any man would want to get in touch with that woman."

Judd suppressed a grin. "Bad first date?"

"Bad? She stole my car and left me stranded in the desert. I had to hitch a ride back to the ranch with the food delivery truck."

He laughed. "What did you do to deserve that?"

"Nothing!" Mason raked his fingers through his hair and scowled. "She just overreacted when I told her she was a lousy driver."

"Wow, you let her drive the Porsche on a first date?"

"*Big* mistake."

"Come on, I want the whole story."

Mason shrugged. "There isn't much to tell. We really seemed to be getting along great at first. We talked nonstop over dinner, found out we both love jazz and hate slow drivers, that sort of thing. And there was some serious chemistry."

"Which caused her to dump you in the desert?" Judd raised a skeptical eyebrow.

"That didn't come until later. After dinner, we decided to check out that little jazz and blues club in town, and we spent maybe an hour there before I got tired of not being able to talk to her over the music. So we decided to drive out to the desert and look at the stars. She told me she had her own names for all the constellations, and she was going to teach them to me."

"That's when you let her drive?"

Mason rolled his eyes. "I figured, why not? Straight desert road, no traffic, what could go wrong? That woman must have set a new record for zero to sixty in a Porsche 911. I think I got whiplash, and she left about a third of my rear tires on the road from all the rubber she burned."

Judd grinned. "Sounds like *your* driving."

"No way I'd drive that recklessly in an unfamiliar car."

"Uh-huh."

A wistful look crossed Mason's face, but he quickly disguised it with a grimace. "That woman is crazy. Damned sexy, but crazy."

"So I guess you won't be seeing each other again?"

"Not in this lifetime."

Judd shook his head, smiling. Mason deserved a little humbling experience now and then. "You paid twenty-thousand dollars to have your car stolen and get yourself stranded in the desert. Claire sounds like my kind of girl."

And speaking of his kind of girl, he had to find Lucy, make sure she hadn't decided to hunt down Buck herself. "I'll catch you later, man. Call me on the cell phone to let me know if you need help tracking Buck."

Outside, the evening festivities were getting started. A country band was setting up on one side of the ranch, while a top-forty band was already playing on the other side. Two beer tents had been erected, and a mechanical bull had been brought outside for the bull-riding contest later. Judd just hoped it wasn't going to be naked bull-riding.

Guests were milling around, some already more than drunk enough to party Fantasy Ranch-style. As he stood on a rock path, trying to imagine where Lucy might have decided to go, a couple came darting out from behind the bushes, buck naked. Oblivious to Judd, they kept running, not a stitch of clothing in sight. Judd stopped in his tracks, shaking his head as he assured himself that he hadn't just hallucinated.

Clicking footsteps came from behind him, and then a familiar voice. "Did you see that couple?"

He turned to find Lucy. "The naked one? How could I miss them?"

She giggled. "I just flushed them out of the bushes, trying to find Buck."

"So you've already heard he's missing. You shouldn't be bothering with this. Relax and enjoy your vacation, what's left of it."

"Yeah." Her expression sobered. "What's left of it."

He took her hand. "We haven't talked about what will happen after."

"Let's don't." She smiled, but it looked forced. "Let's just have fun while it lasts."

If he weren't mistaken, she seemed pretty upset at the idea of them parting ways, and Judd had to admit that he was, too. But she was pretending otherwise. She wanted him to think she was immune to any romantic entanglement between them. It was all an act—she wasn't simply the seductress she pretended to be. She was much deeper than that.

It seemed crazy, a woman as beautiful as her not

understanding the power she had over men, but with Lucy anything was possible. He remembered the picture on the mantel in her living room, of a conservatively dressed woman he could hardly recognize as Lucy at the time.

But now he could see that woman clearly in Lucy. It was her cautious side, the one she was trying to ignore here at the ranch. She was exploring a new persona on her vacation, wearing new clothes and trying new things. Lucy had found her wild side, and he liked it.

To hell with respectability. To hell with all his resolutions about settling down with a nice boring girl. To hell with staying away from Lucy.

If she didn't want to talk about the future right now, that was fine. He could wait.

"How about we grab some carry-out from the restaurant and sidestep all these crazy festivities?"

Lucy frowned. "Claire's acting really strange. I've never seen her in such a bad mood. I think I should hang out with her tonight."

Judd swallowed his pride and nodded. "Sure, that sounds like the right thing to do."

He stared after her as she walked away. Just when he thought he had Lucy all figured out, she went and confounded him again.

LUCY DIDN'T WANT to think about leaving, but her last day on the ranch had finally arrived. She rolled over and glared at the sunlight flooding in the window. Claire was sleeping on the fold-out bed nearby, having spent the night in Lucy's suite. It was so unlike

Claire not to go out and party at every opportunity, but she hadn't wanted to talk about her bad mood.

The curiosity was driving Lucy crazy. She couldn't wait to hear about the disaster date. "Claire? You awake?"

Her friend rolled over and peered at her with one eye open. "Is it morning already?"

"Mmm-hmm. When are you going to tell me what happened on your date with Mason?"

Claire made a face and exhaled, covering her eyes with one forearm. "It was a disaster. What else do you need to know?"

"You'd never let me get away with giving you so few details!"

Lucy sat up and swung her legs off the side of the bed, determined not to move until she'd found out what had turned Claire into a pouty shell of her former self.

There was a long pause, and then she began. "Most guys I go out with, I spend the whole first date deciding how I'll be able to keep them under my thumb. With Mason, I completely forgot to do that."

"Isn't that a good thing?"

Claire peeked out from under her arm. "Not if he's a jerk."

"How did you go from being completely relaxed with him to thinking he's a jerk?"

"I came to my senses. I'd just been temporarily blinded by lust, or great conversation, or whatever."

"What, exactly, happened between all that great conversation and sexual attraction, and you deciding that you hate him?"

"We'd had this fabulous evening together, and in the middle of the desert he decided to let me drive, since I'd told him about my love of cars. He got quiet as I started driving, and it gave me a chance to think."

"About this fabulous guy you've just had a fabulous date with," Lucy filled in.

"No, about how googly-eyed I'd been over him all night. That's the worse mistake a woman can make with a guy—letting him think he has the upper hand. So I decided to assert a little control. And that's when he insulted me, and I had to kick him out of the car."

Lucy bit her lip to keep from making any comment. Claire was such a control freak, she'd actually sabotaged her chances with a guy just because she liked him too much. She couldn't handle that out-of-control feeling that came with falling for someone.

"Tell me you didn't kick him out in the middle of the desert."

Silence.

"Claire!"

"It wasn't the *middle* of the desert."

"Please say he at least had a cell phone to call a cab."

Claire shrugged.

"I think you owe him an apology."

"He called me a lousy driver!"

"That's a reason to put his life in danger?"

"He survived, didn't he?"

"How did you get him out of the car, anyway?"

Claire flashed a wicked grin. "He thought we were stopping to look at the stars together."

"You're an evil woman, Claire."

"Okay, I'm evil. I have to file down my horns with sandpaper at night. Now can we drop the subject?"

Her behavior had been harsh even for Claire. Lucy was shocked to realize that maybe her friend actually needed some dating advice from her for once. But she knew when to stop pushing Claire. Lucy needed time to strategize her next move.

"I hear there's a group of calendar guys showing up at the ranch today, I think in about a half hour. Want to go check them out, get a few autographed calendars to take home?"

"I guess."

"You guess? Muscle-bound men are going to be here, and you *guess* you'd like to see them?" Claire's foul mood was even more serious than she'd thought.

Lucy hopped out of bed, heading for the bathroom. "Get up and get ready!" She peeked out the bathroom door after a moment, catching Claire still in bed. "Come on, I hear they do a strip routine. If we don't hurry, we'll miss it!"

A half hour later they were both ready and headed out the door, but what Lucy found in the hallway was Judd with his fist poised to knock.

"Hey, you're still here."

"We were just leaving."

"I'm supposed to be keeping an eye out for Buck, making sure everything runs as planned today, but I've gotta eat sometime. Care to join me for breakfast?"

Now that the case was pretty much wrapped up, Lucy supposed Judd was free to dress in his own clothes all the time. No more bimbo cowboy suit. Lucy was going to miss it. She was going to miss *Judd*, she realized, angry at herself for letting such thoughts invade her mind now.

He wore a pair of faded khakis and a white Oxford shirt with the sleeves rolled up to midarm, and he looked sexier than ever. She smiled when she looked down to see that his feet were clad in a comfortable old pair of brown Top-Siders. Why did she have to be such a fool? Why did she have to fall for a guy that was supposed to be her one-night stand, a guy that didn't even know the real her?

"Actually we're going to check out the calendar hunks that are headlining today."

Judd's smile turned into a grimace. "I'll pass."

Claire had gone on ahead of them in the hallway, so Lucy whispered, "I'm trying to cheer her up. If she gets interested in the beefcake, we can leave her to have her fun and go grab breakfast."

He nodded, the amusement returning to his eyes, and followed them out of the hotel and across the main plaza, following the signs pointing the way to the hunk-o-rama. They were about to enter the tent when Lucy caught a flash of six-foot-tall tanned skin and long chestnut hair passing by.

Buck!

Claire had already found her way to the table full of calendars for sale. Lucy grabbed Judd's hand and pulled him outside. "It's Buck! This way!"

Judd pushed ahead of her.

"I think he went toward the saunas!" Lucy called to him, following behind.

A minute later Judd came back, shaking his head. "No sign of him."

An uproar back at the beefcake tent caught their attention, and they went to check it out. Inside, a group of sumo wrestlers stood on stage, puzzling over the calendars.

A flustered announcer was saying, "I apologize, ladies. It appears we've had some kind of mix-up. I'm sure the men you're waiting for will be here any minute now."

Women were cursing, throwing calendars on the floor, milling out of the tent. "What kind of lousy resort is this?" a passing guest muttered.

Judd and Lucy looked at each other knowingly. Buck was behind this. Possibly his best trick yet. Lucy tried not to laugh at the puzzled wrestlers, but a giggle came bubbling up, then another.

"We'd better let Mason know about this. I have a feeling Buck canceled the calendar guys, and there are gonna be a lot of angry women roaming the resort today."

By the time they got to the administration area, a cluster of disgruntled women had already gathered to report their displeasure over the missing calendar hunks.

"What the hell's going on out there?"

"Our saboteur has struck again, this time with a band of sumo wrestlers."

"What?"

Once Mason had been informed of the latest events, he sent Lucy and Judd out to look for Buck. They were wandering through the crowd outside, discussing where he might be likely to strike next, when a commotion at the pool caught their attention. Judd took off running, and Lucy followed.

A crowd of women had gathered. At its center were the rowdiest of the bunch, women chanting, jumping up and down, waving their panties in the air.

Judd made a move to shove his way through the crowd, but Lucy stopped him. "This looks a little dangerous. Are you sure you want to go in there?"

He cocked his head. "What is it that they're chanting?"

Lucy strained to listen over the music of the nearby band playing. "Big Boy? No. Big Buck? We want our Big Buck."

"Buck!" they exclaimed simultaneously.

"If he's in there somewhere, I think we should hang back, wait until he busts out to catch him."

"Maybe you're right," Judd said, shaking his head at the melee. "Looks like Buck's fan club finally got out of hand."

The crowd was moving to the west, away from Judd and Lucy, nearing the edge of the pool. They edged their way closer, keeping an eye out for anyone breaking free of the throng of women. And just when Lucy was beginning to wonder if Buck was still alive in there, she spotted a dark form huddled down to the ground, emerging from a forest of legs. He dove into the pool, swimming beneath the water and surfacing on the far side.

"Judd, the pool!"

But Buck's fan club spotted him again before he could get away. Wearing a pair of bikini briefs, one boot, and what looked like a shirtsleeve, Buck made it only a few feet from the pool when a whole new epicenter of women formed and swarmed him, picking him up and carrying him away.

"Yikes, we'd better save him. Call security!"

Judd started to dial, but before he could finish, security guards came running from all directions. Breaking their way into the crowd, they fended the women off as best they could. Lucy took off in search of medical help.

Five minutes later the mob of women had dispersed. Buck was lying on the ground, soaking wet and nude except for one sleeve of his shirt, getting checked for damage by the resort doctor. Judd shook his head at the scene, and Lucy stared in disbelief. Here and there upset Buck fans stood crying at the sight of their fantasy man lying in ruin.

"I wonder which lucky gal got his underpants."

"I don't want to know."

"Guess you're lucky that wasn't you," Lucy finally said. "I heard you were developing a fan club of your own."

"Me?" He grinned. "A fan club of one, I hope."

Lucy felt her face turn red. "Yeah, I guess there's at least one member."

They walked back to Mason's office in silence, sobered by the day's events. Once there, Mason listened as they described the out-of-control mob, Buck's failed escape and his subsequent rescue.

"I guess everything finally conspired against Buck. His very own fan club getting out of control, probably all women angered by the absence of the calendar hunks.''

"And that was his doing, too. I bet he never guessed his sumo wrestler stunt could have such dire consequences.''

"Wow, Buck and Natasha, huh? You think she paid him off?''

"It's possible," Judd said.

"He did just buy a new Corvette last month, and I've heard rumors that it was a gift from a rich girlfriend. Maybe that was Natasha." Mason shrugged, and they all sat silent for a moment before he spoke again. "Thanks for your help, guys. The police are going to question Buck after he's been patched up."

Lucy and Judd stood to leave.

"I just have one question, Mason," Lucy said. "Is there any chance of you and Claire seeing each other again?''

His expression darkened, but he shrugged. "Do I look like a masochist?''

"I'll take that as a no," Lucy said. She had a theory about why Mason and Claire's date had gone so terribly wrong—they'd met their match in each other, and neither one of them had been ready for it.

Judd closed the door to Mason's office. He and Lucy were alone in the hallway. This was it. Lucy had her own man problems to deal with now.

"We did it. What'll we do to celebrate solving this case?''

Lucy cast her gaze down at the tile floor. He looked so happy, so carefree. It wasn't the right time to make her confession, but there wouldn't be a right time.

And she couldn't wait any longer. She had to tell him she was a fraud before he started liking her any more than he already did.

"Judd, I have to apologize to you."

"No, don't say another word. I know I've given you a hard time, but you've been a big help to me these past few days."

"I have?"

He grinned. "Well, that, and you're pretty easy on the eyes, so I haven't minded having you around quite as much as I would've had you believe."

"That's not what I meant, though."

Lucy felt her heart breaking, splitting wide open. She'd foolishly let herself fall in love with Judd Walker, and she was afraid he had feelings for her, too. But not the real her. He was attracted to the woman she'd been pretending to be for the past week, a woman that was nothing like the real her.

Without her new hair and wardrobe, Lucy wouldn't have had a chance with a guy like Judd. She didn't have a chance. Not if she came clean.

"I have to go. I think Claire wants to leave today. It's been a fun week, but I don't expect us to see each other again."

His expression instantly hardened. "What are you saying?"

"The time we've had together was great, but I don't see it leading anywhere."

"Lucy, if you're worried about—"

"Let's don't ruin a fun week by arguing now." She felt the tears coming. She wouldn't cry in front of him, not now. "I have to go."

She turned and walked away without looking back.

# 13

HE WAS A FOOL. He'd done it again. He'd let a woman he knew was dangerous have his heart and stomp all over it. It was his own fault. He'd known from the beginning that Lucy was trouble, and he'd gone ahead and fallen for her anyway.

He had no one to blame but himself. He tossed items of clothing into his suitcase without bothering with neatness, cursing himself the entire time. Lucy was gone, and he was alone, and it made him mad as hell.

He bent to pick up a pair of shoes, and caught a glint of something purple beside the bed. Closer inspection revealed it to be Lucy's handbag. She must have forgotten it in his room recently.

His investigative nature getting the best of him, he opened it up. Inside was a tube of lipstick—Passionate Plum—a bottle of sunblock, SPF 15, a Fantasy Ranch guest pass, expired as of tomorrow and a wallet, obviously just the one she was carrying especially for the resort, because it contained only fifteen dollars cash and a photo ID card.

The woman in the photo hardly looked like the Lucy he knew. A clean-scrubbed face shining with natural beauty, light brown curls refusing to be tamed by a ponytail holder, a smile that was open and honest and genuine. She looked the way she had in the photo on her mantel. It was the innocent Lucy, the one that kept teasing him from behind the sex-kitten image. He spent so much time trying to figure out which was the real Lucy, he had failed to appreciate the fact that they were just two parts of the same smart, beautiful, sexy, real woman. Lucy herself didn't even understand that fact.

He knew why she felt she had to leave now, and he had to convince her that she was wrong.

JUDD KNOCKED on the door of Lucy's suite, but no one answered. He tested the lock and then burst inside, looked around at the scene, and amazed himself by not even blinking. Claire lay sprawled on the bed, surrounded by dessert plates, some half-empty and some untouched. One of everything on the room service dessert menu, it looked like.

"Where is she?"

Claire glared at him. "Gone, you fool. Couldn't you have figured out a way to keep from making her miserable?"

"That's what I'm trying to do."

She spooned a glob of ice cream and hot fudge out of the sundae she was working on and popped it into her mouth, then spoke around the mouthful. "Lucy left an hour ago, caught the bus back to the city, saying something about how she never should have used you the way she did. The girl's delusional."

"Used me?"

"Like I said, delusional."

"I thought you were leaving, too."

She scoffed. "Look at me! Don't I look like I could use a long vacation?"

Lucy had lied, then. She'd left because of him, not Claire. "I just want to find her and tell her how I feel."

"And you couldn't do that before she got her heart broken?"

"I tried. She left before I got the chance." And now he might never have the chance. He wanted to kick himself for not coming to his senses sooner.

"I suggest you find her to tell her what an idiot you are and ask her if she can ever find it in her heart to forgive a fool as big as yourself."

"Don't you think you're rubbing it in a little hard?"

A mischievous half grin played across her lips. "She won't answer her phone or her door—I can pretty much guarantee it—but you can find her at the office sometime next week."

"Thanks. I owe you."

Claire sighed and jabbed her spoon into the hot-fudge sundae. "You'll have to excuse me now, I'm busy."

"Excuse me, Miss? I need to book a cabin in the mountains as soon as possible."

Lucy had Mr. Jameson, a long-time client of the agency, on the phone as she copied down the man's needs for his upcoming Caribbean vacation. And now there was this bozo that didn't even have the manners to wait for her to finish her phone call before demanding her attention. She'd been dealing with jerks like that all day, and she'd had enough.

Without looking up from her writing, she covered

the phone receiver with one hand and muttered, "You'll have to wait until I'm finished here."

"No problem. I can wait all day for a pretty lady like yourself."

*Oh, great, he's a lecherous sleaze, too.* But something about his voice sounded familiar. Very familiar.

Too familiar.

She looked up from her notepad, temporarily pausing her scribbling. *Judd.* His voice had been obscured by a mock Texas drawl. He was wearing a white Stetson and a denim shirt with faded Levi's.

Her cowboy fantasy had come to life. Again.

And here she sat, looking nothing like the Lucy Connors he'd known at the Fantasy Ranch. Pretending to be someone else may have given her some newfound confidence, but she hadn't seen any point in continuing to pretend to be someone she wasn't. Now she wished she'd at least bothered to put on some lipstick, wear her hair down or find a more stylish outfit than the boring old thing she'd pulled out of the closet that morning.

Now Judd would see her the way she really was, and she wouldn't blame him for hating her. But she still wanted to run away.

"So what do you say? Me, you, a remote mountain cabin for two, a few weeks of uninterrupted bliss."

On the phone her client continued, "and we'll need a suite in St. Thomas for three nights..."

"Excuse me, Mr. Jameson, there's a problem here at the agency. I'll call you back later this afternoon." She said goodbye and hung up before he could object.

"Is that a yes?" Judd looked even better than she remembered, and they'd only been separated for a week.

"You shouldn't have come here." Lucy felt her heart rate quicken as she stood from her chair and looked for an escape route.

The mailman and his giant bag of mail were blocking the front door, and an elderly couple thumbing through cruise brochures created a barrier to the rear exit. Her only hope was to slip into Claire's office and lock the door, then climb out the window. Desperate times called for desperate measures.

But just as she began to edge away from her desk, Judd said, "Lucy, please don't run off again. There's a lot I need to say to you."

There was something in his voice that kept her from moving. She turned back to him and forced her gaze to meet his.

"I'm really busy. I don't have much time to talk."

"Already taken care of. I got permission from the boss to steal you away."

Strange, he didn't even seem to notice that she'd turned back into a boring wallflower.

"But we're three travel agents short—" She looked toward Claire's office, but Claire's replacement for the week, Yvonne, was standing in the doorway waving Lucy away.

"Go!" she commanded.

"But..." She turned back to Judd, and he extended his hand to her.

Silently she slid her hand into his and let him lead her away from her desk, away from her giant pile of work, and out the front door. That was when she saw the antique horse-drawn coach waiting in front of the agency. It looked as if it had just rolled off the page of an old Western novel, and she got a giddy feeling inside when Judd led her to it, then opened the door for her to step inside. The driver turned and tipped his cap to her before she disappeared into the velvet recesses of the passenger compartment.

Inside, the noise and heat of suburban Phoenix nearly melted away, and there was only the two of them. Lucy smoothed the fabric of her gray flannel skirt over and over again, determined not to look into Judd's eyes. She didn't want to see his disappointment yet.

"Where did you find a stagecoach?"

"Old West Days going on a few blocks down."

She stared out the window. "You shouldn't have gone to all this trouble."

"Well, Miss Lucy. I see you're gonna make this proposal a hard one for me, and I suppose I deserve it."

Lucy blinked. "Proposal? Of wha..." Her voice died. He couldn't mean what she thought he meant.

"I'm getting ahead of myself here. I've got a lot to propose, if you'll just give me the chance."

Now that she knew the real Judd—ex-cop, private investigator—seeing him in his cowboy getup seemed ridiculous. And heartwarming. He'd gone to all this trouble for her, when she was nothing more than a liar and a coward. But not for long. It was time for her to come clean and to let him know who the real Lucy Connors was, uptight frumpiness and all.

Wincing as the coach hit a bump in the road, Lucy finally looked Judd in the eye. Amazing how he managed to hide his shock at the difference in her appearance.

"I'm not who you thought I was at the ranch." She made a sweeping motion toward herself to indicate her altered appearance.

"What do you mean?"

She reached into her handbag and rummaged around, looking for evidence of the real her. She pulled out her daily planner. "Look here at my schedule. Monday at five o'clock, go to the library for live reading of *A Gardener's Memoirs*. Monday at seven o'clock, home to wash curtains and dust light fixtures. Monday at eight o'clock—"

"Lucy, why are you reading your schedule to me?"

"Don't you see? I'm not at all the person I pretended to be on vacation. I deceived you. I don't go country line dancing. I don't own any zebra-print underwear or black string bikinis. I've never even worn red lipstick before last week...I've never really done anything fun until last week."

She felt tears welling up in her eyes as she realized how true her last statement was. She'd always played it safe, she'd always been afraid to let loose, to go after anything that seemed remotely dangerous. Like Judd.

He was shaking his head. "I don't know what you're talking about, but it seems to me you're making a big deal out of nothing. I don't care what your underwear looks like. That's not why I love you."

"You what?"

The coach hit another bump, jarring Lucy out of her seat and across the aisle into Judd's lap. Before she could right herself, Judd grasped her arms and pulled her up so that she was next to him, pressed against him, on the small bench seat.

"I love you."

She felt as if she were still tumbling, falling, head over heels. Judd Walker loved her? It seemed impossible, but there he sat with that very emotion clear in his eyes. This was even worse than she'd thought.

"But don't you understand? You don't love me, you love the woman I pretended to be. You love Wild-and-Crazy Lucy, and I'm just boring, old, pays-her-taxes-three-months-early Lucy."

"I know exactly who you are."

"No, I'm so sorry I deceived you, Judd, but I'm not what you want." She twisted her hands from his grasp and leaned out the window of the coach. "Driver! Stop right here please!"

"We're not finished."

Before he could stop her, Lucy pulled open the door and climbed out. They'd made their way into the thick of the Old West Days festival. She glanced around for the best getaway route, but already a crowd of curious children had gathered around the coach, interested in the horses and the odd means of transportation.

"Hey, can we pet your horses?" one little boy called.

Lucy peered past him, spotting a gap in the crowd. She went for it.

"Lucy, wait up!"

She heard Judd's footsteps behind her, but as soon as he made it down from the coach, the children flocked to him.

"Hey, mister, are you a real cowboy?"

"Can we pet your horses?"

"Is that lady an outlaw you're trying to catch?"

"Do you have a gun?"

Lucy didn't stick around to hear Judd's responses. She congratulated herself for wearing sensible shoes and took off at a fast walk, enveloped by the crowd before Judd could escape the throng of children. She skirted food stands and craft tables, without any idea where she was headed.

Up ahead the crowd grew thicker, and the sound of poorly sung country music filled the air. On a small stage stood a man and woman singing a duet of an old Kenny Rogers and Dolly Parton hit. Lucy loved the song, even sung badly, and she couldn't help stopping to listen. Here was as good a place as any to hide from Judd.

If he had any sense at all, he would just give up and go home. That's what the brave new Lucy wanted him to do. Yes, of course it was.

Then why did her heart feel as though it had just lost its one big chance for love?

Selfishness, that's all it was. She wanted Judd for herself, though she didn't deserve to have him. Not when she was a liar and a fake.

She felt tears begin to well up in her eyes again as she listened to the couple on the stage crooning lyrics that suddenly sounded sad. She blinked back tears and stood to leave. She should be at work now, not hiding out at the Old West Days feeling sorry for herself.

And that was when the singing stopped.

"Excuse me. Sorry to interrupt, but I really need to

find someone out there in the crowd. Lucy Connors, are you out there?"

She turned back to the stage, and there was Judd. He'd commandeered the microphone in spite of the protests of the displaced singers. The band's playing had halted. The audience began to make noise, whispering, calling out song requests. People looked around, hoping to spot the mysterious Lucy.

"Hey, sing us a little Johnny Cash," the tipsy woman next to Lucy called.

Ignoring the crowd, Judd took a deep breath and continued, "Lucy, I know you're out there, so please just listen to me. I know you're more than what you wear or how you style your hair. Can't you understand that I saw past all that? I didn't fall in love with how you look, I fell in love with who you are."

A man in the audience yelled out, "Yeah, man, we love you, too!"

"But I pretended to be someone I wasn't," Lucy whispered to herself. "I was a fraud, and a liar, and you didn't deserve to be treated that way."

Judd continued. "Lucy, you were yourself on vacation, and you're yourself now. Maybe I understand you better than you do, have you ever considered that?"

She frowned and shook her head.

"Everyone has a wild side. Some people, like you, just need a little more effort to draw it out."

Could he be right? Could she really have a wild side she'd always been too afraid to explore until Judd showed up handcuffed to her bed?

It made so much sense, she didn't know why she'd never realized it herself.

She stood on tiptoes, waving her arms to get his attention. "I'm over here!"

Audience members around her cheered. Judd looked in her direction, spotting her finally. He handed the microphone back to a singer and ran off the stage.

Lucy pushed her way through the crowd, meeting him halfway. He caught her in his arms and held her there.

"I love you, Judd."

He squeezed her tighter, planting soft kisses on her forehead. "I need to hear it a few more times."

"I love you, I love you, I love you."

"Just needed to be reminded why I put on another damned cowboy outfit."

"For me?" She looked down and saw that he was wearing boots, too.

"The boots especially. Just for you."

# Epilogue

JUDD LOOKED OUT over the orange-red desert, wind whipping at the back of his head. The setting sun had painted the sky in shades of pink and purple almost too bright to be real. He hadn't been to this spot in more than three months. It was his favorite place in all of Arizona, a scenic lookout point where one could see for miles and miles, where hills and mountains spread out forever and the sunsets were always breathtaking.

He usually came here to hike or to just sit and think, but lately life had been so busy, consolidating households with Lucy, dealing with the extra cases he'd picked up from all the publicity over the Fantasy Ranch sabotage case, fighting to gain the respect of Lucy's ornery cats—who still weren't too keen on giving him any bed space at night—he just hadn't had time.

Not that he minded his new life. On the contrary, he loved it. Life with Lucy might not have been the calm, boring, ordinary existence he once imagined for himself, but it was everything he wanted.

A small hand snaked around his waist and interrupted his reverie. "If we don't hurry up, the minister's going to blow away."

Their minister, a small frail man in his seventies, did appear to be struggling to remain upright in the wind.

Lucy wore a long white dress that showed off her

sexy figure, wisely foregoing a veil or any fancy hairdo in deference to the gale that always swept through the desert at this time of year. She looked more beautiful today than ever.

"What are we gonna do about those two?" He nodded toward their attendants, Mason and Claire, who hadn't spoken civilly since a certain Porsche theft months earlier.

Lucy smiled. "I've got a plan."

"Uh-oh."

"Just listen. What if we invite them both on our trip to Hawaii next month, but don't tell either of them the other is going?"

"And then what? Tie them together with a bunch of those Hawaiian flower necklaces and leave them until they make up?"

"It's Hawaii, the most romantic place on earth, and they're perfect for each other. All they need is a little helping along."

Judd pulled her close. "That sounds like a dangerous plan...but I like it."

She shushed him when Mason approached.

"Break it up, you two. We've got a wedding to get on with here." Mason thumped Judd on the back and gave Lucy an affectionate wink.

"Leave the lovebirds to their little romantic moment, you jerk." Claire, the most windblown bridesmaid in history, appeared from behind them.

She and Mason hadn't even seen each other since their twenty-thousand-dollar date. Judd guessed the problem was that Mason had finally met his match, and his pride was still smarting from the battle of wills that ensued.

"You two have to get along for the next fifteen minutes," Lucy warned.

"No problem. I'll just wait until after the ceremony to push him off the cliff."

A few feet away, the minister's toupee caught on the wind and went sailing away. He scowled after it, and Judd took that as their cue to get started before anything more important blew off into the desert.

He led Lucy to the spot where the ceremony would take place. Claire and Mason followed behind them and took their places.

"Dearly Beloved, we are gathered here today..." the minister began.

Judd looked into Lucy's eyes, seeing in them a lifetime of joy they would share. Falling in love with Lucy had been amazing, but this moment, right here and now, was where the real adventure began.

**THE BAD GIRLS Club**

*They're strong, they're sexy, they're not afraid to use the assets Mother Nature gave them....*

Venus Messina is...
### #916 WICKED & WILLING
by Leslie Kelly
February 2003

Sydney Colburn is...
### #920 BRAZEN & BURNING
by Julie Elizabeth Leto
March 2003

Nicole Bennett is...
### #924 RED-HOT & RECKLESS
by Tori Carrington
April 2003

*The Bad Girls Club...where membership has its privileges!*

**Available wherever**

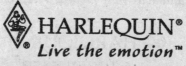

HARLEQUIN®

*Temptation.*

**is sold....**

HARLEQUIN®
*Live the emotion*™

**Visit us at www.eHarlequin.com**

**When Suzanne, Nicole and Taylor vow to stay
single, they don't count on meeting these sexy
bachelors!**

## ROUGHING IT WITH RYAN
January 2003

## TANGLING WITH TY
February 2003

## MESSING WITH MAC
March 2003

Don't miss this sexy new miniseries by Jill Shalvis—
one of Temptation's hottest authors!

*Available at your favorite retail outlet.*

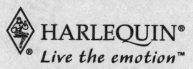

If you enjoyed what you just read,
then we've got an offer you can't resist!

# Take 2 bestselling love stories FREE!

# Plus get a FREE surprise gift!

# COMING NEXT MONTH

### #913 LIGHTNING STRIKES Colleen Collins
*The Wrong Bed*

The chances of Blaine Saunders's beautiful brass bed being delivered to the wrong address *twice* are about the same as lightning striking twice. Even more surprising, while searching for her missing bed, she ends up in the wrong bed with the right man—the very sexy Donovan Roy! Sparks fly between them, leaving her to wonder if lightning will strike three times....

### #914 TANGLING WITH TY Jill Shalvis
*South Village Singles #2*

Nicole Mann has no time for romance so she's vowed to remain single. No problem. So what's she to do with the too-charming-for-his-own-good Ty O'Grady? Especially because the man won't take no for an answer. Fine. She'll seduce him and get him out of her system...or is it get her out of his system? He has her so confused she hardly knows what day it is! One thing is for sure, *this* is temporary. Or so she thinks....

### #915 HOT OFF THE PRESS Nancy Warren

Tess Elliot is just itching for the chance to prove herself as a serious reporter. All she needs is a juicy story. So when the perfect story practically falls in her lap, Tess is all over it. But rival reporter and resident bad boy Mike Grundel wants in on the action, too. Of course, Mike isn't only interested in reporting...getting under Tess's skin is just as much fun. But it's getting her under the covers that's going to take some work!

### #916 WICKED & WILLING Leslie Kelly
*The Bad Girls Club*

Businessman Troy Langtree is making some changes. After his latest fling ended in disaster, he decided to start over—in a new city, in a new job. He's hoping he'll be able to focus on what he wants. Only, once he sees bad girl Venus Messina sunning herself on the balcony, all he wants is *her*. After all, every man knows that bad girls are better....

HTCNM0103